how to be a goldfish

T0398662

how to be a goldfish

Jane Baird Warren

Cover illustration by
Julie McLaughlin

Scholastic Canada Ltd.
Toronto New York London Auckland Sydney
Mexico City New Delhi Hong Kong Buenos Aires

Scholastic Canada Ltd.
604 King Street West, Toronto, Ontario M5V 1E1, Canada

Scholastic Inc.
557 Broadway, New York, NY 10012, USA

Scholastic Australia Pty Limited
PO Box 579, Gosford, NSW 2250, Australia

Scholastic New Zealand Limited
Private Bag 94407, Botany, Manukau 2163, New Zealand

Scholastic Children's Books
Euston House, 24 Eversholt Street, London NW1 1DB, UK

www.scholastic.ca

Library and Archives Canada Cataloguing in Publication
Title: How to be a goldfish / Jane Baird Warren ; cover by Julie McLaughlin.
Names: Warren, Jane Baird, author. | McLaughlin, Julie, 1984- illustrator.
Identifiers: Canadiana (print) 20220182825 | Canadiana (ebook)
20220182833 | ISBN 9781443192309
(softcover) | ISBN 9781443192316 (ebook)
Classification: LCC PS8645.A76673 H69 2022 | DDC jC813/.6—dc23

Cover art copyright © 2022 Scholastic Canada Ltd.
Image on page 235 by Alexia C. Roy

Text copyright © 2022 by Jane Baird Warren.

6 5 4 3 2 1   Printed in Canada 114   22 23 24 25 26

For Frédérique and Gabrielle

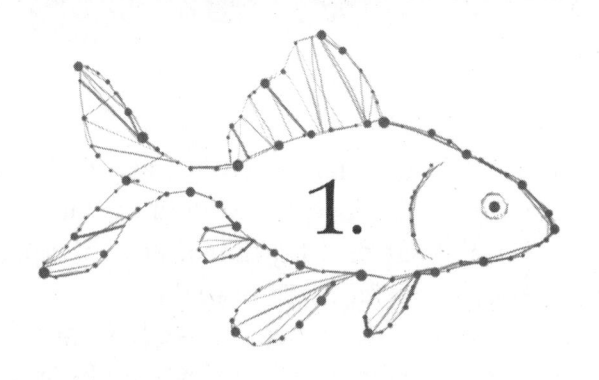

1.

Lizzie

I bet there aren't many kids who can say social studies changed their life, but it changed mine. It really did. If it weren't for social studies, Harry's farm would be history, and I would have never figured out who David was. He'd be just some city kid who passed through Scotch Gully one day in May.

It was last period and I was busting for school to be over so I could get outside. The grass was thick and green; the gullies, those hillside ditches that gave our town its name, were still fat with spring runoff; the sky was blue and cloudless; and at Harry's, the ewes were due to lamb any day. Harry was the closest thing I had to a grandfather, and great as he was, to him I was still a kid. So when he said I could name the first lamb born, I knew he expected a cute little-kid name like Curly, Fluffy or Snowflake, but I had my own ideas.

1

For a ewe lamb, I'd narrowed it down to *Baa*-rbra or Tina *Baa*-llerina. Harry wouldn't get it, but I thought it was hilarious. I grinned, just thinking about the look on his face when I told him.

That grin disappeared when I walked into social studies and saw the maps pulled down and covering both sides of the chalkboard. Those maps rolled down like that meant we were about to have a pop quiz. By the time I took my seat, kids were buzzing like a nest of angry yellow jackets.

"Settle down," Miss Gambacort said. "It is not a quiz."

"Then what is it?" Gordon McInnis asked.

"A special project."

Gordon groaned so loudly he sounded like a cow in a branding chute. "Ah, c'mon, Miss G," he said. "Please don't make us sit in the library. It's way too nice to be stuck inside."

"You won't need the school's encyclopedias for this project, Gordon."

Miss G walked to the world map. She pulled the chrome handle down, then let it go. The map rolled up into its case smooth as corn silk, and that's saying something since that map had been around so long that some of the countries had new names.

Underneath that map in blue chalk, it said, EVERY FAMILY HAS A HERO.

I guess that's true. Grandfather Ross — my

mom's dad — died fighting in World War II, and my grandma lost three uncles in World War I.

"I want you to discover firsthand that history isn't just dates and places in a textbook or encyclopedia. History happens to people. Each one of you," Miss G said, "will interview a family member. Your assignment is to find out what their life was like and uncover the challenges they faced."

I put up my hand.

"Yes, Lizzie?"

"Can we write about someone who's not alive anymore?"

"No. It has to be someone you can actually interview."

Reluctantly I pointed at the chalkboard. "But that says 'Every family has a hero.'" Miss G tipped her head to the side like she didn't understand. She was new to Scotch Gully so maybe she didn't know about me yet. I picked my next words carefully. "I've only got two people in my family — my mom and grandma. They're great and all, but they're not very interesting. Or heroic."

As soon as the words were out of my mouth, I regretted them. I knew better than to draw attention to my family. I looked around the class expecting the worst. To my surprise, most people's heads were nodding, as though they were thinking the exact same thing about their families. I guess that made sense. How were any of us supposed to find a hero in our tiny town, where most folks were farmers and have been for generations?

"I think you'll be surprised, Lizzie. Class, it's 1981. We have televisions and microwave ovens. Some of you may even have a VCR. But your parents were born in the 1940s, when those things didn't exist. Some houses didn't even have indoor plumbing. Ask your grandparents what it was like to use an outhouse when it was minus twenty degrees."

I didn't see how using an outdoor privy in the winter made someone a hero, but I didn't want to invite trouble by drawing even more attention to my family, so I kept my mouth shut this time.

"You look doubtful, Lizzie," Miss G said. "What do you think makes someone a hero?"

"I dunno," I answered. "Fighting in a war, I guess."

"Good. Any other ideas, class?"

"Pulling someone from a burning building," Gordon said.

Kids started calling out more answers: saving folks from earthquakes, tornados, tidal waves, and all manner of natural disasters, none of which had ever happened here in Scotch Gully. Like I said, this isn't a place for heroes.

"Those are all fine ideas," said Miss G. "Can we agree to call them action heroes?"

"Yeah! Like Han Solo," Gordon called, and the class started buzzing again. A whole year after *The Empire Strikes Back* came out, and the boys in my class were still nuts for Stars Wars. It's all they talked about on the school bus. That and hockey.

"Settle down, class." Once things got quiet, Miss G explained, "Not all heroes leap into the fray. There are quiet heroes too. People who take a stand to protect the weak or to right a wrong."

"Like on the news last night," Carolyn Cousins said. I like Carolyn. Her dad and grandad were the county vets, and she liked animals as much as me.

"Explain, Carolyn."

"Well, it said on the news there was going to be another rally in Toronto this afternoon, because of those three hundred men who got arrested in February for being gay, and because of how badly the police treated them. My dad said Margaret Atwood gave a speech at the last big rally. So people like that, who try to help, would be quiet heroes, right?"

"Exactly, Carolyn," Miss G said, then she pointed right at me. At least I thought so, but it wasn't me she was looking at. It was Bethany, in the desk behind me. Bethany Budge is what my grandma calls a piece of work. She's had it in for me for as long as I remember. I try to avoid her, but that's not easy. Scotch Gully is a small town, and our school is even smaller.

"Yes, Bethany?" Miss G asked.

"My grandmother says all the gays are going to Hell."

BAM. Just like that, in the space of a finger snap, the whole classroom went silent. All eyes were on Miss G, waiting to see what she'd do. She took a deep breath and held it in like she was counting to ten, which is exactly what my grandma tells me to do when I'm upset.

Finally, she spoke. "You've all heard of Nellie McClung, Rosa Parks and Gandhi?"

Everyone nodded.

"Well, they were also protestors, and now we call them heroes. But I think we've strayed, class. Let's get back to your projects."

I wished I could see Bethany's face right then, but I didn't dare turn around. Instead, I kept my eyes fixed on Miss G as she picked up a piece of chalk and wrote INTERVIEW on the board in big letters.

"A good interview will reveal something about your subject that you never knew before, and that is what I want you to write about. One student will be chosen to represent our class and share their report on Parents' Day."

Parents' Day is a huge deal. By the time everyone's brothers, sisters, parents, grandparents, aunts, uncles and cousins show up, it feels like all of Scotch

Gully is squeezed into the school gym. I couldn't imagine anything worse than standing up on that stage in front of the whole town, talking about my family and reminding folks of the very thing I wanted them to forget.

Nope. I could never do that. It would be like trying to put out the last coals of a campfire with a can of gasoline. But I had nothing to worry about on that score. My project would be dull as dirt — my mom was only a small-town lawyer, and my grandma was just a part-time librarian.

Miss G moved across the front boards to the map of North America and pulled the handle down. When the map rolled up into its case, new instructions were revealed, written in green chalk this time.

SHARE YOUR HISTORY: CREATE A FAMILY TREE.
- Trace your family back to when they came to this country (or as far back as you can).
- Show their names and explain how they are related to you.
- The Scotch Gully Mercantile has stocked poster board especially for our class.

That was thoughtful. It meant nobody's mom or dad would have to drive all the way to the Woodward's in Arbroath County.

Then I noticed the very last line.
- All family tree posters will be hung in the gym for the Parents' Day assembly.

Oh no!

"Psst. Psst, Lizzie Ross."

Bethany Budge. I fixed my eyes on the chalkboard, hoping she'd take the hint and leave me alone. Hard to believe now, but back in kindergarten I desperately wanted to be Bethany's friend. At church on Sunday, the Budges take up two whole pews. Bethany has five older brothers who always seem to be bossing her around, teasing her or ignoring her. But they stick up for her too. When she wears her hair Princess Leia–style, with her braids wrapped around her ears like two cinnamon buns, or on the school bus when she talks like Yoda, no one, not even Gordon McInnis, dares make fun of her. Those Budges might fight amongst themselves, but they take care of their own.

I wanted a big family like that so badly it hurt. Between polio and two world wars, there are only three people left in my family. I mean, I love my mom and grandma, I do, but it's always just the three of us at home, and sometimes the quiet feels thick and too heavy. Back in kindergarten, when I asked Bethany to be my recess buddy, she made a face and said, "My gran says I'm not allowed to play with you." Then she shoved me. It wasn't hard, but I was so startled, I fell down and landed on my backside.

"Hey, Lizzie Ross," Bethany said now in a voice

low enough not to attract the teacher's attention. "I'm talking to you."

I wished with all my heart that Bethany would just hush up, but I'd never been able to wish Bethany Budge away. It's like Grandma always said, "If wishes were horses, then beggars would ride."

"I can't wait to see your family tree," Bethany whispered. "Do you even know who your father is?"

I tried to swallow, but my spit had dried up. When I didn't answer, she leaned so far across her desk that I could feel her breath on my neck. It smelled like warm egg salad with too many onions.

"My gran says you're a bastard," Bethany whispered. "She says your mom's hippie ways are a bad influence on the whole town."

I should have turned around and faced her then. I should have defended my mom and told Bethany to shut her mouth. But I didn't. Some dogs drop their tails and slink their bellies low when you catch them out. Other dogs are fighters, stand their ground, and growl like they've got angels behind them. Bethany was like that. A fighter. Calling her out would only have made things worse.

My hands clenched and unclenched. I tried counting to ten, but I only got to three before Bethany spit-whispered again.

"My gran says in the old days, bastards like you got adopted out to real families."

I knew I shouldn't let anything Bethany said bother me. I knew she was just being a mouthpiece for her grandmother. But I couldn't help it — it hurt. I blinked really fast to make the tears stop. Then, like it was the most important thing in the world, I opened my notebook and copied all the project instructions word for word.

When the school bell finally rang, I grabbed my stuff, shoved it in my backpack as fast as I could and ran for the school bus. I had to get a front-row seat. Not even Bethany Budge would dare pick a fight within earshot of Mr. Carson, our bus driver.

* * *

I'd been taking the same bus ride since I was five years old. Usually, I loved looking out the bus window and noticing the small things along the way; each fall as the leaves changed to orange, yellow and red; the way winter snowfalls left mounds like winter beanies on top of everyone's mailbox; and the return of the turkey vultures each spring circling high above the fields and gullies. But after what Bethany had said, I didn't see anything. All I wanted was to get to Harry's farm. I needed to feel the sun on my face and smell the grass and apple blossoms, the manure and new leaves.

The stop-sign arm swung out, and the school bus doors opened. As soon as my feet hit the ground, my chest started to fill with air like I'd been holding my breath, and I could finally breathe. That first gulp tasted of apple blossoms. I drank it down. The petals had begun dropping the week before. Soon they'd be gone, and when that happened, Harry would announce that it was time to start making manure tea. The only thing I'd be smelling on the farm then would be sheep poo. Harry claimed that manure tea was the secret to his prize-winning vegetables, so every year I helped him by collecting bags and bags of ewe berries — a.k.a. sheep poo. Then we shovelled, stirred and strained that poo into manure tea.

"That's life on a farm," Harry always said. "Some things stink, but others are downright beautiful."

Today had been a stinker. I needed a little dog love.

"Expo," I called, as I walked to the farmhouse. *Where was he?* He usually met the bus, tail wagging, and walked with me up the long drive. "Hey, Expo!"

There was still no sign of him by the time I reached the front pasture. Just the ewes grazing, their bellies fat with baby lambs. It wouldn't be long now.

I was almost at the farmhouse by the time I spotted Expo, and when I did it almost made me forget about Bethany. Expo was riding behind Harry on the ancient tractor, tongue out and paws up on

Harry's shoulders as the tractor bounced, groaned and growled its way along. The tractor pulled an old trailer, the one Harry made ages ago, back when my mom was a kid and used to come here after school like I do now. Today that trailer was piled high with willow switches. I knew what that meant — Harry and Expo had been down by the creek.

Expo barked when he saw me, and Harry slowed the tractor way down. A few years ago, Expo would have just jumped off while the tractor was moving and raced toward me. These days he waited for it to almost stop before he climbed down, careful to look for footholds at every step. He was limping again, favouring his right side. My worry must have shown on my face because Harry called, "He's okay, Lizzie. He's been chasing rabbits all afternoon. He's just knackered."

Harry's good like that, saying things a person needs to hear. I smiled a thank you, then asked, "Did he catch any?"

Harry shook his head. "Those rabbits get quicker every year." That was to make me feel better too.

"Looks like a good willow harvest, Harry. I'll help you unload and sort." I wasn't ready to talk about school yet.

"First, we'll have our snack."

"On the porch?"

"Of course. Now off and wash your hands."

Harry put the tractor in gear. It moved, coughing and belching, round the back of the house to the old cast-iron bathtub that Harry found at the town dump a few years back and dragged home to soak his willow branches. He called that taking the spite out of the willow.

I left my backpack on the porch, then headed inside to the kitchen sink. Expo was close on my heels; he knew what was coming next. If the smell of fresh-baked zucchini bread made my mouth water, Expo would be leaving a snail-trail of drool all across Harry's clean floors.

In the kitchen, two fresh loaves sat on a wire rack beside the stove. After I washed up, I readied a tray with two plates, two glasses, a jar of last year's apple jam and a pot of butter. I cut three slices of zucchini bread and put them on a plate — one each for me, Harry and Expo. But Expo's never been much for waiting. He was headbutting my leg. Greedy old thing.

"I'd never forget you, boy," I said, scratching him behind the ears where he liked it best. "Aw, what the heck." I sliced him an extra piece and fed it to him quick before Harry got back. "Don't tell on me."

I took a carton of milk from the fridge, added it to the tray and carried everything out to the porch. By the time I got there, Harry was already climbing the porch steps.

I always liked this part of the day. Just Harry and me sitting together still and quiet, listening to the frogs and crickets. I didn't want to spoil that by talking about my trouble at school, so I said, "So, Harry, how long did it take you to get that old tractor started this time?"

"A little longer each year," he answered. "But nothing that a little duct tape, a lot of patience and one of Mrs. Macrath's hairpins can't fix."

Harry was always naming things around the farm for Mrs. Macrath. Those hairpins, the heavy black roasting pan that was big enough to cook a whole piglet, the beat-up white coffee percolator with three blue cornflowers on the side that he claimed made the world's best coffee, the upright piano in the parlour and even the enormous enamel tub we used when it was time to wrestle Expo into a bath. Harry called them all Mrs. Macrath's *this* and Mrs. Macrath's *that*. When I was little, I imagined that there was an enormous Mrs. Macrath Factory somewhere in the city that made it all.

"Better not lose Mrs. Macrath's hairpin, Harry, or you might have to use your bodkin next time you need to clean the spark plugs."

Harry pretended to look horrified, and I laughed some more. Harry's bodkin was precious. It's the tool he used to make his willow furniture.

"You know, Lizzie, I could teach you how to

make baskets. You could sell them with me at the farmers' markets. That's what your mother did back when she was your age and came here after school." One corner of Harry's mouth turned up in a half-smile. "That mother of yours," he said, shaking his head slowly from side to side, "was mad for horses. Making willow baskets was how she saved enough to get one. It could be a good way for you to start saving."

"Saving for what? I don't want a horse."

"There must be something you want, Lizzie. Everyone's got some secret wish."

I did, it's true. But I could sell a thousand baskets and make a pile of money and never get any closer. My secret wish wasn't something you could buy. What I dreamed about was sitting around a Thanksgiving table, elbow to elbow with brothers, sisters, aunts, uncles and cousins. Or filling up an entire church pew with my very own family.

Thinking about my secret wish made me think about school and having to hang our family tree posters in the gym for Parents' Day. I hated knowing it would remind folks how different my family was from theirs, and I worried that Bethany's gran would start up her back-fence talking about Mom and me again.

I looked up at Harry. He was looking right back at me.

"Did something happen at school today, Lizzie?"

I nodded. Harry always could tell when I was chewing on a problem.

"I've got some trouble, Harry."

While I dug out my notebook from my backpack, I told him everything Bethany had said. Then I opened the book to the page where I'd written the instructions for the social studies assignment. I handed it to Harry. He read it. Slowly.

When he was done, he set it in his lap and said, "Oh dear."

"You see how bad this is, right? I don't know anything about my father or his family. Bethany Budge has already started taking pokes, and it's not like I can talk to Mom. She doesn't think there's a problem. She'd just tell me to hold my head high and say, 'Our family has nothing to be ashamed of.' But, Harry, I'm not that brave."

"You're plenty brave, Lizzie."

I shook my head. "Mom's brave. She doesn't care what folks say or think."

"That's true. But I sometimes wonder."

"Wonder what, Harry?"

"Well, has your mother been able to make those brave choices as an adult because of how safe and secure she felt growing up here?"

"You mean because she never had to explain why her dad wasn't around?" I shrugged. "I guess you're right. Everyone in town knows that Grand-father Ross died in the war. Plus, it's plain as white bread that her parents were married. Grandma was a Sinclair when she left Scotch Gully and a Ross when she came back."

Harry didn't say anything at first. But his fore-head got all wrinkly. He looked out over the fields, and I wondered if he'd spotted a ewe in trouble. Finally, he said, "I'm sad to say that around here, that still matters. Being different can be hard, Liz-zie. That's something I understand all too well."

"Is that why folks around here don't know about how you grew up?"

Harry had told me his story not long after I started school and had my first run-in with Bethany Budge. He said it was the first time he'd told anyone in years. Not even my mom or grandma had heard it before then.

Harry nodded. "I wanted to fit in. I didn't want to give people in town a reason to talk. I suppose you and I are the same that way."

He was right, but I still had a problem. For kids in my class, making a family tree was no big deal. Scotch Gully was the kind of place where folks married right out of high school, and most stayed together even when they fought like cats and dogs. Here, family farms were passed down from generation to generation, sometimes with three generations living under one roof. Not my family. Grandma headed west after high school, and her only sibling was an older sister with polio. There was no one to take over, so her dad sold off the land. Now all that's left of our farm is the house. And all that's left of our family is me, Mom and Grandma. I'm the only weirdo in town. Well, me and Harry.

"What am I going to do about this?" I asked, pointing to the page in my notebook where my family tree sat almost empty, but full as I could make it.

"I might just have an idea or two."

"Really? That would be great because the only idea I had was not doing it. But that's not an option. Can you imagine what my mom would say if I didn't hand in my homework?"

"I believe she'd have kittens," Harry said, chuckling. "Lizzie, remember those stories I told you about when I was a little boy in England?"

Mom says my face misbehaves before my brain kicks in. I guess she's right because I was halfway through what she'd call a teenage eye-roll when Harry started to chuckle. "I gather by that look on your face that you're not interested in hearing my story again."

"Sure I am, Harry. It's just . . ."

"It's just that you don't see what this has to do with your school project." He chuckled again. "Stay with me, Lizzie. When I was very little, I travelled along with a pair of street performers. My job was to soften up the punters — the audience — so they'd loosen their wallets. All I needed to do was look like the pitiful child I was. My earliest memory is being propped up at the side of a road and given a tin cup to rattle while she sang songs or told fortunes and he played the fiddle or did magic tricks and, yes, even picked some pockets."

"I remember, Harry." I also remembered that this part of Harry's life was not nearly so cheery as he was making it sound now. I've heard him tell a different version of this story where he was cold and always hungry, all because his mom — the person who was supposed to protect him — traded him for a bottle of alcohol when he was just a year old.

Harry said, "I was with those performers almost three years. I knew their act inside and out. And while some of it became dull, like seeing the same skits and hearing the same songs over and over, I never got tired of watching them do magic."

"Harry, how does any of this help me?"

"Magic."

"Aww, Harry . . ."

I couldn't hide my disappointment. He smiled, then leaned forward and ruffled my hair.

"Do you know how magicians do what they do, Lizzie?"

"I know it's not magic."

"Fair enough," Harry chuckled. "But have you heard of misdirection?" He stretched his right hand to the side, reaching as far over the porch railing as he could go. "A magician will do something over here," Harry said, wiggling his fingers. Then suddenly, he pointed to the orchard, his eyes all wide and surprised looking. I turned around to see what he was looking at, but there was nothing there. When I turned back, he was holding the last piece of zucchini bread.

"Misdirection," Harry said and waggled his eyebrows. "While you were busy looking where I was pointing, I had time to take this." Expo's head was on Harry's knee, and he was staring at that zucchini bread, looking hopeful and pitiful at the same time. Harry broke off a corner and fed it to him. "Expo wasn't fooled, were you, boy?"

"Okay, Harry. I get what misdirection is, but how's that going to help me?"

"How about this for a start?" He took my notebook and turned to the page where I'd tried to fill in my family tree. Five names. That was all I had. Right beside the box labelled *Father*, Harry made a neat fold in the page, making my father's side of the family tree disappear.

I had to admit it solved a big problem. I couldn't have filled in those boxes. Even my mom didn't know much of anything about my father's family.

"But, Harry, people are still going to notice. It won't stop the gossip."

"Then add more misdirection. Keep their eyes so busy and entertained looking at your mother's side of the family that they don't have time to notice what's missing."

"Entertained how? A family tree is just a chart with names and dates."

"It can be whatever you make it, Lizzie. To start, you could put in pictures."

Pictures were a good idea, but for the misdirection to really work, I'd need something more. Stories might work . . . if they were good ones.

I've always liked the story of Grandfather Ross. The way Grandma told it he was a real Scotsman, only one year off the boat and seeking to make a name for himself in this country when war broke out. Grandma had just left Scotch Gully and gone west to join her sister. When she stepped off the train in Vancouver on Dominion Day, July 1st, 1940, she saw Phillip Ross standing on the platform looking dashing in his uniform. Grandma said their eyes met, and they both just knew. It was love at first sight.

But Grandfather Ross had already enlisted. He knew he might have to ship out any day, so he didn't waste a minute, and just ten short days after they met, he got down on one knee and proposed. They married at city hall the very next day. Soon after, he got his orders and shipped out overseas. And not too long after that, Grandma found out she was pregnant with my mom. Then, tragedy happened. Grandfather Ross's plane got shot down over Italy. He never got to meet his daughter, and my mom never got to meet her dad. Sort of like me — I've never met my father either. The difference was Mom's dad was a war hero. I'm pretty sure mine wasn't.

Grandma said my father got drafted into the American army but didn't want to fight in Vietnam, so he ran north to Toronto. My mom explained it differently. She said my father didn't believe in wars and fighting. She called him a conscientious objector. But I watched the CBS news, and that's not what Walter Cronkite called those guys. He called them draft dodgers. My dad must have been an expert dodger. He didn't just dodge the draft. When my mom told him she was pregnant, he dodged that too. My dad packed his bags and moved to Amsterdam. That was almost fourteen years ago. We haven't heard from him since.

That was definitely not a story I'd put on my poster board for the whole town to see. I knew stuff like that shouldn't matter in 1981 — at least that's what my mom said — but Scotch Gully was an old-fashioned, everyone-goes-to-church kind of place. Still, I thought this whole misdirection thing might work if I could collect enough good stories about my mom's family. Grandma had some uncles who fought in World War I. I could work with that.

"Harry," I said. "You're a genius. I know exactly what to do."

"What's that, Lizzie?"

"I'm going to make little story scrolls and attach them to the poster board. Then people can unroll each one and read it. No, wait! I've got an even better idea!" I was getting excited. "I'll make little doors in the poster board that open, and behind each door will be that person's story. People will be so busy opening all the doors and reading all the stories they won't notice what's not there."

"I'd say you've got a winner of an idea there, Lizzie. Now, how about you take Expo and collect the eggs?"

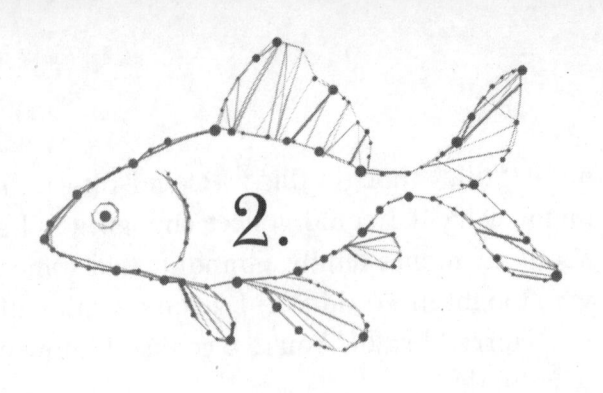

2.

David

Meanwhile, sixty kilometres south and west of Scotch Gully, in the heart of the city, David Macrath sat in his classroom at Rosehill Public School, willing the school day to be done. Even though he stared at the red second hand of the classroom clock as it jerked from one second to the next with an almost audible click, it still seemed to David that the closer he got to the end of the day, the slower the time moved. That was always the way, especially when you were really looking forward to something. And there was nothing David was looking forward to more than leaving Rosehill Public School and moving back home. To pass the time, David picked up his pencil and started to doodle. Usually, he drew R2-D2, C-3PO, Jawas or stormtroopers — anything from Star Wars. Not today. Today his doodles had four legs and fur.

"David. David MACRATH!"

David's head snapped up. His teacher was standing right in front of his desk. "Whoa," he mouthed. *How the heck did she get there?* The last time he'd noticed her, Miss Torrente had been writing on the board. She was like a ninja, he thought, except ninjas don't scowl or tap their fingers, *peck peck peck*, on your notebook.

"That is a dog," Miss Torrente said, still tapping. "You are supposed to be writing down the homework from the board, not drawing pictures of dogs. You know what I'm going to say now, don't you?" She lifted a hand in the air and snapped her fingers once. "Class?"

All around him, fingers started to snap. First, it was just a few kids, then pretty soon everyone was snapping. *Snap. Snap. Snap.*

"What are your classmates telling you, David?"

"Snap to it," he grumbled.

Miss Torrente cupped her hands around her ears. "I'm sorry, David. What did you say?"

"Snap to it," David repeated, louder this time. It was, he'd learned in his four months at Rosehill, the only way to make the snapping stop.

His teacher lifted her arm high in the air, and just like that, everyone in the classroom stopped snapping. Miss Torrente, David thought, would be a heckuva dog trainer.

"Hurry and write down your homework, David."

"No," he said a little too fast and a little too loud.

"I beg your pardon?"

He never meant to be smart-alecky. Except for the whole finger-snapping thing, he thought Miss Torrente was okay.

"It doesn't matter," David tried to explain. "I'm moving back home and won't be here anymore."

All around him whispers fizzed and bubbled, like when you twist the lid off a soda bottle. David knew not to look at Marty right then, but he couldn't help it. Sure enough, Marty was staring right at him and sliding a finger across his throat. *Uh-oh.*

Miss Torrente dragged his attention back. "Home?" she asked.

"Back to Cabbagetown. To my grandad's old house."

It had been only a few weeks since his grandfather died. Talking about him made David's eyes swim. Just then, the bell rang and David was spared the embarrassment of crying in front of his classmates. Chairs scraped. Kids headed for the back of the classroom to grab their bags and jackets. David tried to stand up too, but Miss Torrente had her hand on his shoulder. She waited like that, with a hand holding him in his chair, until the room was empty. Then she lifted her hand from his shoulder and crouched down beside his desk.

"I was very sorry to hear about your grand-father's passing. You must miss him very much."

David nodded. With the back of his hand he wiped away tears. Miss Torrente fetched a box of tissues from her desk and handed them to David.

"Are you sure you're moving today, David?" she asked.

"My mom and I decided after the funeral. She knows I'll be happier there."

"I'm sorry to hear that. You haven't been with us long. I'll miss having you in class, but I understand. It's been hard for you here, hasn't it?"

David nodded. He took a tissue, wiped his eyes, then blew his nose.

"Okay, then. Wait right here. I'm going to the office to check on your situation."

The second Miss Torrente was out the door, David ran to the coat hooks at the back of the room. He was too late. His backpack was gone. He hurried to the door. If he was lucky, it would be in the hall. Sometimes, when Marty and his goons were too busy with basketball to plan something really rotten, they would slide his backpack down the corridor like it was a curling stone, or unzip it, shake everything out on the floor, then dump the empty pack on top. David looked up and down the hall. It wasn't there.

I should have kept my big mouth shut, he thought.

If only he'd just written down the homework when Miss Torrente told him to, and never, never, *never* said that he was moving. Now that those creeps knew he wouldn't be around much longer, they were going to get creative.

Before Miss Torrente returned, David had slipped on his jean jacket and hurried outside to look for his backpack. He had to find it; his entire collection of Star Wars action figures — some of them gifts from his grandfather — was inside.

David spotted Marty right away. Marty was on the basketball court playing HORSE with his gang. They'd dumped their school bags and jackets behind one of the nets. David scanned the ground looking for his backpack, but it wasn't there. Maybe that was good news. Maybe this once he wouldn't have to run around chasing it like some dumb palooka while Marty used it to play monkey in the middle. The bad news was, he still had to find it.

"Where is it?" David called. No one answered. No one even looked up. "Where's. My. Backpack?" he yelled.

Marty tucked the basketball under his arm. "Hey, guys, look who it is! It's Cheetos. Hey, Cheetos, wanna play HORSE?"

David got called a lot of names on account of his hair. Carrots. Matchstick. Ginger. Flame. But the name he hated most was Cheetos.

David glared at Marty while he worked out what to do next. It's not like he could fight him. Marty was huge for a sixth-grader. He had hands the size of most kid's heads, feet like flippers, and he was mean. David never understood why Marty had it in for him. Still, his time at Rosehill had taught him that if he didn't want to get wedgied, swirlied or thumped, he'd better do what Marty said.

That was before. But knowing Marty and his bully crew would never be able to ambush David in the washrooms ever again was different.

With newfound courage, David made his demand. "Give it back."

Marty acted innocent. "Give what back?"

"My backpack. Give it."

"I don't have your backpack, Cheetos."

Marty's goons laughed like that was the funniest thing in the world.

"I'm not playing around. I know you guys took it. I want it back. Now!"

"Then go get it, Cheetos," Marty said. He pointed to the basketball net on the far side of the court.

David's backpack was stuck inside the basket, ten feet in the air.

"Go on, Cheetos," Marty said. "All you have to do is shinny up the pole."

David couldn't shinny up the pole, just like he couldn't climb a rope in gym. Everyone knew that.

"Well?" Marty said.

When David didn't answer, Marty shoved him. Any other day that shove would have been David's signal to run, but not today. Angry, with his jaw tight and his teeth clenched, he faced Marty and demanded, "Get it down! Now!"

"Careful, Marty," one of Marty's goons called. "Looks like Cheetos is gonna to lose it." They all laughed like a pack of hyenas after a kill.

When David still didn't move, Marty said, "Come on, guys. Let's go. If Cheetos isn't even going to try, where's the fun?"

Marty turned to leave. As he walked away, he pulled something out of his pocket and waved it in the air. Boba Fett. The special pre-release action figure that David got before *The Empire Strikes Back* came out. He'd had to collect four proofs-of-purchase cards, tape a five-dollar bill to the order form and mail it to Kenner toys. It took every nickel he'd saved. It was the pride of his collection, and there was Marty, waving it in the air as he walked away.

Something inside of David snapped. Head down, he ran full speed at Marty, tackling him from behind. Marty landed face down on the pavement with a loud *thunk*. David heard a satisfying *ooof* as the wind was knocked out of his tormentor. In a flash, David was on top of him, pounding Marty for every rotten stinking lousy thing he'd done and said since David arrived at this snooty school four months ago.

Pound.

For every time Marty had called him a fairy and a white-trash loser.

Pound pound.

For every time Marty had shoved him, knocked him down, got him in a headlock, stole his backpack.

Pound pound pound.

For . . . everything.

Fist in the air, poised to deliver another blow, David froze. Marty was messed up. His chin was split and he had a broken tooth. *I did that?* David thought. *If Grandad was alive, he'd be so disappointed in me.* He choked back a sob. David hadn't wanted any of this. He'd never wanted to leave his grandfather's house or go to a school where he didn't know a soul. He'd tried to make friends, but from that first day in January, everyone had avoided him. Lonely and needing someone to talk to, David had called his grandfather.

"I want to come home, Grandad. I hate it here. Please can I come home?"

"Oh, David." His grandfather had sounded sad and lonely too, but he'd said, "Stick it out. Your mother thinks your new school will be better for you. Most of those kids go on to college or university. She wants that for you."

"But, Grandad, they all hate me. I don't have any friends. I don't even have you anymore."

"You will always have me, David. You can call me every day. In the meantime, try finding someone who likes the same things as you. What about Star Wars? You love Star Wars."

By the end of that phone call, David had promised his grandfather he would try harder. The next day he'd brought all his Star Wars collectibles to school, and it had almost worked. Until Marty stepped in, ensuring no one dared play with David.

As he sat there, straddled across Marty's back, David wondered for the gazillionth time what he could have done to make Marty hate him so much. And for the gazillion and first time, David had no answer.

Just then, he felt a hard yank on the collar of his jean jacket. He twisted around to see who it was. Miss Torrente! She was yelling and trying to pull him off Marty. David twisted free, snatched Boba Fett from where Marty had dropped him on the pavement, and ran.

He ran as fast and as hard as he could. He ran until his chest burned and his legs felt like Jell-O, but he still didn't stop. *Just a little farther,* he told himself. Just a little farther, to Yonge Street and his mom's office — a shop front with Rosehill Realty painted in big black letters across the glass. If he could just get there . . .

* * *

David heard the sirens when he reached Yonge Street. *They're coming for me because of what I did to Marty*, he thought. Panicked, he looked around for someplace to hide, but this part of Yonge Street was all brick and cement, sidewalks and storefronts. There wasn't a decent tree to climb or bush to duck behind. Five police cars came flying past with lights flashing and sirens screaming.

Five police cars? Marty must be dead! He stuck his hands up in surrender like the criminals did on TV, but the police cars zoomed past, heading south toward Bloor Street, where they quickly set up a blockade across the intersection. Beyond the intersection and the police cars, the street and sidewalks were jam-packed with people holding signs and marching. That's when David understood that the police weren't interested in him. It was another protest march. David hadn't paid much attention to them before — he'd had bigger problems — but he knew there had been lots of marches, protests and demonstrations since the February riots.

Feeling stupid, David lowered his hands and hurried on to his mom's office. He was too old to believe in wishes, and his prayers had never worked. If they had, his grandfather wouldn't be dead, and

David, his mom and his grandad would all still be living together in the Cabbagetown house. David and his grandfather would spend long summer days together visiting the animals in the High Park Zoo or swimming at Sunnyside pool. In winter, they'd go skating on Grenadier Pond or at Nathan Phillips Square. Then there were the lazy, comfortable days when they'd stay home and watch old Tarzan movies on TV, read comic books or just talk. Instead, for the last four months, David had sat alone after school in a walk-up apartment, waiting for his mom to finish work.

Just in case, as David pushed open the door to Rosehill Realty, he sent up a prayer that his mother was back from the lawyer's and the two of them could leave right away for Grandad's house — his new–old home. He was pretty sure it wouldn't work. But it couldn't hurt.

His mother wasn't at her receptionist's desk. The rest of the office was empty, except for one realtor talking on the phone and another one who was flipping through a big red book and making notes. The man on the phone saw David and pointed to Kelch's office. His mom must be inside with him. Cameron Kelch.

David didn't like his mom's latest boyfriend, and he was pretty sure his grandad hadn't liked him either. When his grandfather was still alive, he used to whisper to David, "Don't you think he looks like Lurch from *The Addams Family*?" That always made David giggle, but secretly he thought Kelch was more like Grand Moff Tarkin from Star Wars — tall and thin as a streetlamp, with an oversized head, slicked-back hair and a beak for a nose. David wasn't sure if all kids annoyed Kelch or if it was just him, but ever since he and his mom moved in, David had made a point of staying out of Kelch's way as much as he could. It wasn't easy. The apartment was small, and the only way David could avoid Kelch was to hide in his room. Which he did. A lot.

His first month in Kelch's apartment, David had tried complaining to his mom. "He's not my dad. He shouldn't act like he is."

But his mother seemed to like that about Kelch. "I know he's not perfect," she'd said. "But he has your best interests at heart. It was his idea that we move in with him so that you could be in a better school district. He wants to be a role model for you and show you how to be a successful young man."

"I already have a role model — the best role model in the world: Grandad," David had answered.

His mother had sighed. "Yes, David. Your grandfather is a good man. I'll never forget how kind and gentle he was with my mother, and let me tell you, that wasn't easy. Your grandma Maeve was a difficult woman. Especially at the end of her life. But,

David, Cameron is a good man too. He wants to be involved. In fact, he's planning to sign you up to play football this spring. He'll even help coach."

"But I don't like sports."

"Cameron says all boys should play sports."

"I don't care what he says. I like movies and comic books and stuff like that."

"Please, David."

"I like what I like, Mom."

"For my sake, give this a try? There aren't many men willing to take on a woman with an eleven-and-a-half-year-old."

David hated it when she said stuff like that. Like he was a burden. He also hated the way his mom acted around Kelch — like everything he said was sooo smart. It made David nuts. Just because she never went to university and Kelch did, that didn't make him any better than her.

David's mother got pregnant with him when she was in grade thirteen. Back in 1969, most of her teachers were either nuns or priests. Once she started to show, Father Fahey called her into his office and explained he couldn't allow a pregnant unwed teenager to walk the halls of his school. It "sent the wrong message." He explained that the church had a facility for girls like her far away in another city. She was supposed to tell everyone that she was going to her aunt's. After it was over, the church would find a "proper Catholic home" for the baby. Only then could David's mother return home to finish high school. Father Fahey said that outside of marrying the baby's father, this was the only way to protect both her reputation and the school's.

But his mother didn't want to marry at eighteen, and she refused to leave. She wouldn't give David up either. She fought them all — the priests, the nuns and the Catholic school board — and won. David's grandad loved telling that story.

"You should have seen her, David," his grandad said. "I don't think I've ever been so proud as the day your mother got that diploma. Almost nine months pregnant and big as a house, your mother waddled like a duck to the front of that high school gym stuffed full of parents and grandparents. At the sight of her, all those holier-than-thou hypocrites started chittering and whispering so loud you'd think the gym was full of crickets. Then your mother turned around with her diploma clenched tight in her hand and she faced that whole gym — stared them all down as fierce as anything. I wish I had that sort of courage, Davey. It would have been a whole different life for me if I did, but I could never be that brave."

"But, Grandad, you were a soldier. You fought in the war alongside the Americans and the British. Your division took Juno Beach!"

His grandad shook his head and said, "That's a whole other kind of brave, David." David had never understood what he meant.

Kelch had two university degrees framed and hanging behind his desk so they would be the first thing people saw when they walked into his office. The wall across from his desk was covered with framed photos and newspaper articles — action shots of Kelch playing football and basketball, and pictures of him on sports teams lined up behind oversized trophies. To David, Kelch was no different than the kids at Rosehill who wore those expensive shirts with crocodiles on the chest like a commercial, advertising how rich they were. Kids like Marty, who swapped stories about family trips to Hawaii, Disney World and Whistler, and then went swimming in each other's backyard pools. David had never been outside Toronto, and he didn't have a backyard pool. Heck, David thought, since he'd moved out of his grandad's house, he didn't even have a backyard. Kelch might not wear shirts with crocodiles, but he brought people into his office all the time where all his sports pictures and university degrees were on show. Different stuff, same sort of bragging, David thought.

"David, you made it." His mom poked her head out Kelch's office door. "I'm so relieved. Did you have any trouble?"

For one uncomfortable second, David worried that she knew about Marty. Then she said, "We've been worried about the demonstrators marching up Yonge Street. Cameron's on the phone with the police about it."

"Mom, can we go to Grandad's house now? I can't wait to get out of here."

"Come inside Cam's office, David. We need to talk."

"Nah," David said. "I'll wait here until you're ready."

"Inside, David. Now!"

He didn't like the sound of that, but it wasn't like he had a choice. He was a kid. He went into Kelch's office, and his mom pulled the door closed behind him, holding one finger to her lips and pointing to Kelch.

"This is ridiculous!" Kelch barked into the phone. "How is anyone supposed to run a business with those nancy boys marching and chanting in the streets outside my door? They're scaring off clients." Then Kelch said, "*They* have rights? What about *my* rights?" and he hung up the phone, hard. "If you ask me, Peter Worthington at the *Sun* had it right when he said they should have all stayed in their damn closets!"

David's mother's eyebrows arched so high they almost touched her hairline. Kelch held both hands up in surrender, then got up, walked over and put his arm around her. "I'm only trying to protect us, Carla," he said. "This place is our livelihood."

She stood stiff as a board, her hands balled into fists, but Kelch didn't let go. Eventually, she relaxed and leaned her head against his chest. Kelch looked over at David and smiled.

Something wasn't right. When David left for school this morning Kelch had been stomping around the apartment, angry that David and his mom would be moving back to the old house. And now, here he was, all smiles.

David's mother pushed gently away from Kelch and turned to look at David.

"David," she said, and he knew he wasn't going to like what came next. People with good news don't have faces that look like they have a stomachache.

"You know that we went to the lawyer today about your grandfather's will?"

He chewed his bottom lip. He hated that his mom was saying "we" and acting like she and Kelch were the team. *It's supposed to be Mom and me,* David thought. He was her kid. Kelch was just some guy she was dating. Some old guy.

His mom took a big breath. "It turns out your grandad didn't own the Cabbagetown house."

"But . . ." David stammered. Of all the things he'd worried about, and there had been a lot since they'd moved in with Kelch in January, this had never been one of them. The Cabbagetown house was his grandad's house. It had always been Grandad's. His mother had even grown up there.

"I don't understand," David said.

"I was surprised too. Apparently, sometime after my mother died, your grandfather sold the house. He's been renting it since then, and now, with your grandfather gone, the man who owns the house wants it back. He's going to fix it up and sell it."

"Can we buy it?" David asked.

"I don't have that kind of money."

"He does," David said, looking at Kelch. It was true. Kelch owned Rosehill Realty, the apartment upstairs and at least a dozen other houses and apartments besides. Kelch liked to brag about how much he owned. He called them his investments and said they were his ticket to his dream — becoming a successful property developer. All he needed, Kelch claimed, was the right piece of land.

"David!"

He shrugged. "So what happens now?"

"We stay here for the time being. And you continue at Rosehill Public School."

David stared at her in disbelief. "I can't go back there!"

His mother and Kelch exchanged a long look. Then she said, "There is some good news."

David shook his head. The only good news would be that they were moving back to Cabbagetown today so he could be near all Grandad's things, smell his smells, sit in his chair. And there was a backyard at the Cabbagetown house. Kelch was always nagging him to turn off the TV and go outside, but there was nowhere to go in that crummy apartment, except the parking lot out back.

Then there was his secret dream. David wanted a dog. In his dreams and doodles, that dog was a big Irish setter with a soft red coat. Since his grandad died, David had decided his dream dog would be called Archie, after his red-haired grandfather. Everyone knows a dog is man's best friend. *If I had a dog*, David thought, *I'd never be lonely again.*

"David?" His mom said his name like she'd asked him a question, but he hadn't heard a thing.

"What?" David said.

"Don't you want to hear the good news?"

"I guess."

"Well, David, it turns out your grandfather owned a farm. I knew he grew up northeast of the city, but I never dreamed that land was still in the family."

"So sell that!" David said. "Sell it, and buy Grandad's house."

"I thought about it," she said. "Cameron thinks it would take too long to sell."

It was too much for David. From riding high on the rollercoaster of hope, only to come crashing down now. The tears he'd fought back in the classroom earlier slid freely down his face. He'd spent all his courage standing up to Marty and his gang of basketball bullies. At school, David had been brave because he believed he'd never have to face them again. The thought of having to return to Rosehill and face Marty was too much. His tears came faster.

"Stop that," Kelch said. "You're too old to be crying."

But David couldn't stop. Especially with Kelch lurching over him with a disapproving scowl. And anyway, Kelch was wrong. David's grandad was a soldier who fought in one of the most important battles of World War II, and he cried sometimes. He cried crazy hard when we moved out, David remembered.

"This is exactly what we've been talking about, Carla," Kelch said. "When you let a boy play with dolls . . ."

"They're not dolls," David spluttered. "They're action figures."

"Enough," Kelch said. "I need you to listen to me, David. For months now, ever since you and your mother moved here, I have tried my best to give you structure, discipline and a positive male role model. Obviously, I've failed. Your attitude, your

inability to integrate with boys your own age . . ."
Kelch shook his head. "And now, since your grandfather's death, your behaviour has been, well, frankly, it's unacceptable. I know you were close to him, but, David, you're about to turn twelve and look at you. Crying and carrying on so much that your mother was willing to up stakes and move the both of you back to Cabbagetown! Well, that can't happen now, can it? But I do have an alternative. I've talked to your mother about this. It's clear to both of us that you need more structure and discipline than we can currently provide, with both of us working full time. And now with a new, very important project on the horizon, we're going to have even less time."

David looked from Kelch to his mother, then back to Kelch again.

Kelch tapped his finger on a pile of shiny brochures stacked on his desk. "I've been explaining to your mother that a good boarding school builds character and would provide you with the structure you desperately need."

"Boarding school? Mom, no!"

"Not now, Cam. Please," his mother said.

Kelch wouldn't let it go. "We've talked about this, Carla."

"This isn't the time, Cam. He's only just lost his grandad."

"You can't keep coddling the boy. Do you want David to turn out like his grandfather?"

David didn't know what Kelch was talking about. All he cared about right then was that he'd never have to go away to boarding school.

"Mom?"

"Think of the benefits," Kelch said. He picked up the stack of brochures. "These are good schools. David would be rubbing elbows with the best people. Not to mention he'd be a shoo-in for any university he chooses."

It was all too much for David. For the second time that day, he lost control. "You can't make me go," he screamed at Kelch. "You're not my father!"

Just then, there was a knock on the door, and one of the realtors opened it a crack. The look on his face showed that he'd heard everything. "There's a phone call for you, Carla," he said. "Line two. It's David's school."

His mom picked up the phone on Kelch's desk and pressed the flashing button.

"This is Carla Macrath," she said. There was a long silence, then she said, "He did what?"

David's mom gripped that handset so hard her knuckles went white. Before it was even back in the cradle, she said, "You got into a fight at school?" But it wasn't really a question, so David kept quiet.

"You hurt that boy, David. He's had to have

stitches, and he's going to need a cap on his tooth. Do you know how expensive those are? What if they expect me to pay for that?"

"But, Mom, he stole my action figures. I had to get them back, and Marty's been picking on me since the first day I went to Rosehill. It was supposed to be my last day, remember?"

David's mother stared at him like he was an alien from outer space. Then David saw her eyes flick toward the stack of school brochures.

"Please, Mom," David begged. "Don't send me away. Please!"

"I'm not sending you away," she said.

Relieved, David tried for one more boon. "I can't go back to Rosehill Public School." He knew Marty would bury him if he did. "I won't."

"Oh yes, you will," his mother said with all the fierceness his grandfather used to talk about. "But not for one week. That was the principal on the phone. You've been suspended."

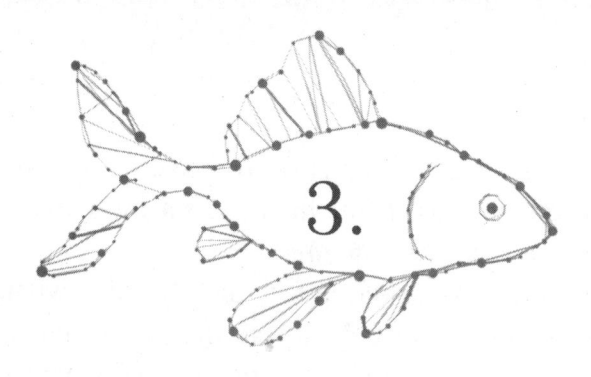

3.

Lizzie

Whoever gets home first makes dinner. That's the rule, and on Monday, that was Mom and me. She lifted a big pot of soup from the fridge and put it on the stovetop with a thump while I fetched the plates and bowls from the dresser.

"Before I forget, Lizzie," Mom said, while she lit the burner, "your grandma will pick you up from Harry's tomorrow. I have to go to Toronto."

"I thought Grandma was working evenings this week?"

"She traded so that I could go to the city."

I don't remember Mom ever going to the city for work before. All her clients were either here in Scotch Gully or next door in Arbroath County.

"How come?" I asked.

Mom stopped stirring the soup and put down the wooden spoon. She walked over to the kitchen table and rested her hands on the back of a chair. She looked serious. Like when she sat me down a few years ago to have *the talk*.

"Do you remember a few months ago when there was a riot in the city? It was all over the news."

"Sure. We just talked about that at school. Carolyn Cousins said there's going to be a big rally in the city today because of what the police did to some men. Some gay men."

"More than some. Almost three hundred gay men were intimidated, threatened and arrested. It should never have happened."

"It's terrible, Mom, but what's that got to do with you?" My mom did small-town lawyering like wills, real estate and small business stuff. She did divorces too, but there weren't many of those around here.

"Well, Lizzie, the people who organized that rally you mentioned want to make sure that what the police did to those men never happens again in this country. So they're putting together a team of people — lawyers, politicians, activists — to make things better."

"But why you, Mom? Aren't there a gazillion lawyers in Toronto?"

"Well, perhaps not quite that many," she chuckled. "But this is why I became a lawyer. And it's what I used to do before you were born. In fact, it's how I met your father."

Hearing her mention my father reminded me of the family tree project. In a gush, I told her all about it — about Harry's misdirection idea, about my idea for making doors in the poster board, and about how Miss G was making us do research.

"You can tell your teacher from me that I think she's brilliant."

"Aw, geez, Mom. I'm not going to tell her that!"

She laughed. "Fair enough. But learning how to research is a great idea," she said. "And I think I can help."

"Really?"

"Sure," she said, fetching fresh napkins from the drawer while I got the cutlery. "We have some pretty interesting documents about our family, thanks to yours truly."

"What do you mean? What do you have to do with it?"

"Fun story, actually. When I was a little younger than you are now, I was mad about *National Geographic* magazines. I devoured them. For a while, my favourite thing to do was to pretend I was an archaeologist on an important dig in some foreign land."

"Really?" My mom worked all the time. It was hard to imagine her as a kid, even harder to imagine her playing. "What did you do? Dig in Grandma's garden?"

"I took a kerosene lamp and a spoon and went down into the old root cellar."

"No way!"

Except for a winter bushel each of apples, potatoes, carrots and rutabagas, we hardly used it. But back in the old days, before my great-grandad sold most of the farmland, they used the root cellar a lot. It's how they got their fruit and vegetables to last through the winter. The floors and walls of our root cellar were packed dirt. The more I thought about it, the more I realized the root cellar would be a good place to pretend you're an archaeologist.

Mom bit back a smile and said, "I probably shouldn't have used one of your grandma's silver spoons as a spade, eh?"

My eyes must have looked froggy because Mom laughed. "Not my best idea, I grant you. Anyway, I went to the back corner of the cellar, where it was darkest. I pretended I was deep inside an Egyptian pyramid. I tipped an old crate upside down and put my lamp on top."

"Then what happened?"

"I cleared away a pile of straw from the corner so I could start digging, and that's when I found it. An old biscuit tin. I was so excited."

"It doesn't sound very exciting." In my head, I was picturing a rusty tin filled with a half-eaten hoard of mouldy shortbread.

"Oh, but it was. When I brought it upstairs to show your grandmother, I was almost dancing."

"What was inside the biscuit tin? What did you find?"

"A collection of very old family records."

"How old?"

"As old as the town. One was dated 1879 from the land registry office in Arbroath County. It was the deed for the land our house is built on."

"That's pretty cool."

"I certainly thought so."

I pictured making photocopies of everything inside that tin, soaking the copies in tea and lemon juice, then baking them in the oven to brown the edges and make them look old. The more I thought about that, the more excited I got. This could totally make up for having zilch on my father's side.

"Was there any other neat stuff in there?" I asked, hopeful.

"Indeed," Mom said. "Every official document belonging to our family was in there, including a last will and testament handwritten and signed by my great-great-grandfather, George Allen Sinclair."

"How come I've never seen any of the stuff?"

"Your grandma kept it out at first. She was pretty excited about having all those old family papers, but she soon got tired of my questions."

"Questions?"

"All those old family documents made me curious about my own father, your grandfather Ross. Your grandma had described him as best she could, but she was thin on details. All she could tell me was that he was born somewhere in Scotland and that he had red hair and freckles, like me. There was a wedding picture, she said, but she'd lost or misplaced it in the move home. I tore the house apart looking for that photo. When I couldn't find it, I searched for a letter or document, something with his name on it, but there was nothing."

"Nothing?"

"Sadly, no. Not even their marriage certificate."

"How come?"

"Well, Lizzie, when your grandma got the news that my father's plane went down over Italy, she was understandably overwhelmed. She decided to come home to Scotch Gully, and we were eastbound on a train the very next day. I expect that when your grandmother packed, she was thinking more about what a four-year-old would need on the long train ride across the country than preserving any photographs and documents. Speaking of those old things," Mom said, wiping her hands on the tea towel, then turning the burner down to its lowest setting, "would you like to see the biscuit tin I found in the root cellar?"

"Yes!"

"Come on. I'll show you," she said and headed to Grandma's room. "Your grandma packed everything up and hid it all on a shelf in her wardrobe, where she thought I wouldn't find it."

"But you did."

"Of course," Mom chuckled. "Secrets rarely stay hidden."

Inside my grandma's wardrobe, on the top shelf, wedged between stacks of sweaters, was a musty old cardboard box. When my mom took the box down, the sweaters tumbled onto the floor. She picked them up and began refolding them.

I looked inside the box. On top lay a jumble of old letters and papers. It was only when I shifted things aside that I spotted a sliver of silvery-grey metal.

"Is that the same biscuit tin?" I asked.

Mom sucked in some air between her teeth. "That's it all right. How about you take that to the dining room table while I put these old sweaters back on the shelf? Then I'll make a salad, and we can have dinner."

I liked the idea of working on the dining room table. There was lots of room to spread out. "Sure. Hey, Mom," I said, picking up the box — it was way heavier than it looked. "Isn't it a little weird that Grandma left all this stuff in a mess like this?"

"What's that, Lizzie?" Mom said with a faraway

look. She was busy picking up those sweaters, re-folding each one and putting them neatly back in the wardrobe.

"Grandma organizes and catalogues everything. Her recipes. Her magazines. Even her seeds. But this is a mess." I tipped the box forward so Mom could see the envelopes and loose piles and papers sliding around. "It's like the shoemaker's kids going barefoot."

I thought for sure she'd laugh at that, or at least think it was clever. Instead, she looked into the box and her eyebrows puckered together. "I see. Well, I suppose she was just too busy back then and thought she'd get to it later. Your grandmother was a single mom, remember? It wasn't easy for her."

"You're a single mom too."

"Indeed, I am. It's still not easy. But I have two amazing helpers; Grandma and Harry both help me look after you so I can work."

Jeez Louise, I was just trying to make a librarian joke about Grandma. Nobody gets me.

Mom said, "You know, when we came back to Scotch Gully after my dad died, it was Harry who stepped in and offered to babysit me."

I knew this already. And as much as I love Harry, I'd had enough serious stuff tossed at me today to last until college.

"Your grandmother would make a terrific person

to interview for your project," Mom said. She folded the last of the sweaters from the bed and placed it neatly back on the shelf in Grandma's wardrobe. "She lost three uncles in WWI, lived through the Great Depression, and lost a husband in WWII." Mom looked sad. "Do you know why she has these old sweaters, Lizzie?"

I had no clue. "I dunno, but I'm pretty sure Grandma wouldn't wear those even to work in the garden."

"That's true enough," she agreed. "When I was little your grandma used to unravel old sweaters like this into balls of wool. Then she'd use the wool to knit socks, hats and mittens for me. She never wasted anything."

"I guess that's why she and Harry get along so good."

"Well. They get along well, Lizzie."

I looked down at Grandma's box so Mom wouldn't see me roll my eyes.

"I just meant that Harry doesn't believe in waste either."

"Ah. Well, you're right about that. And I'd best not waste that good soup your grandma left us by burning it. I'll go give it a stir and make a salad. Dinner in ten minutes?" Mom said and ruffled my hair as she passed.

"Yep."

Back in the dining room, I emptied the cardboard box. First, I lifted out all the loose papers and put them into a pile. Among them were Grandma's high school diploma, some 4-H certificates and a pencil drawing of a dress. Next, I fished out a batch of old cards and letters still in their envelopes. They were addressed to Grandma, so I put them all into a separate stack for her to look at later.

There were only two things left in the box — the biscuit tin and a great big book with a worn leather cover. I lifted out the biscuit tin first and pried the lid off.

The tin was packed full of birth certificates, marriage certificates, death certificates and other things I didn't recognize. What a haul! There was loads of stuff here to use on my family tree poster. Everyone would be so busy looking at all this cool stuff they would for sure forget about my father and his side of the family tree being disappeared. It was exactly the sort of misdirection Harry was talking about.

Next, I took out the big book. It was heavy.

"Mom," I called. "There's a Bible in here."

She stuck her head out of the kitchen into the dining room. "So that's where that went. I've always wondered."

"You've seen this before?"

"Sure. That's the Sinclair family Bible. Open it up."

Sinclair was Grandma's maiden name. Inside, on the first page of the Bible, was a handwritten list of births, deaths and marriages. I scrolled down the list and found my grandma — Emma Eileen Sinclair. Born October 2, 1922.

I called to the kitchen. "Mom, there's no record of Grandma and Grandfather Ross getting married, or when he died. You're not in here either. Neither am I."

Mom poked her head into the dining room. "I expect she never got around to it. Or maybe she found it too difficult, Lizzie."

"What do you mean?"

"Writing something down makes it real."

I suppose she was right. "Do you think we could write our birthdays in here now?" I asked.

"I think that would be fine, but let's ask your grandmother before we do, okay? Now go wash up. It's time for dinner." Mom went back to the kitchen. I heard her clanging around as she doled out the soup.

When I shifted the box to the side I heard the *shhhh shhhh* of something sliding across the cardboard bottom. I looked inside and saw an old paperback novel. It must have been hiding underneath the Bible. The book was thin with yellowed pages, and it smelled musty. *As for Me and My House*, a novel by Sinclair Ross.

Sinclair like Grandma's maiden name, and Ross like Mom and me.

But that wasn't the weirdest thing.

This was a library book.

From the Vancouver Public Library.

All I could think was my always-do-the-right-thing, church-on-Sunday, librarian grandmother didn't return a library book. Holy moly.

I picked it up to show Mom — she had to think this was funny — when an old photograph slid out from between the pages. I knew it was old. It was black-and-white with a wide, ruffly edged border. They don't develop pictures like that anymore. It was a photograph of Grandma.

She was young, maybe eighteen or nineteen years old. She was wearing a white dress like the one in the pencil drawing I'd found, and she was standing next to a freckled boy. Her arm was linked through his. In the picture, she smiled up at him like this was the happiest day of her life. Like she was in love.

Then it hit me — a white dress and a boy with a face full of freckles like Mom. This had to be the picture of Grandma and Grandfather Ross on their wedding day!

After years of wondering what he was like, Mom was finally going to see a picture of her dad. She'd be over the moon!

I flipped it over. On the back, there was handwriting in faded blue ink. It said:

Me and Archie Macrath. Graduation 1940.

Wait. What?

Macrath?

Like Mrs. Macrath's hairpins?

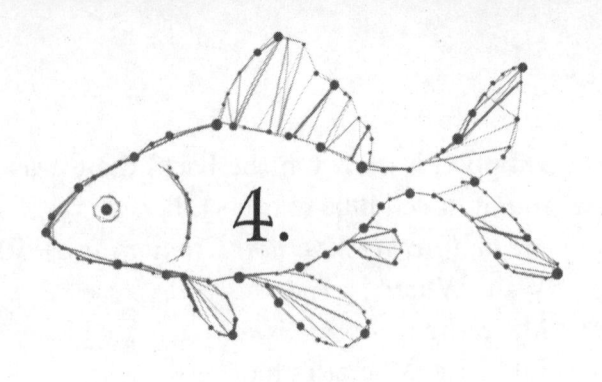

4.

David

David Macrath wasn't only suspended from school; he was grounded too. Except for peeing and eating, he wasn't allowed out of his room. At first, those punishments didn't seem that bad. After all, he was used to spending lots of time in his room, avoiding Kelch. Not to mention that being suspended meant no school, and no school meant no Marty. And so, at first, David happily stayed in his bedroom. He played with his lightsaber until the battery died. He played with his rescued Boba Fett. He read and re-read all his comics.

By two o'clock, David had run out of things to do. Sitting on his bed, back against the wall, he tried to imagine six more days like this and started feeling sorry for himself. He thought about sneaking out to watch TV with the volume turned low, but his mother and Kelch had been taking turns throughout the day to come upstairs and check on him. If Kelch caught him watching TV . . . that would be bad.

He composed a *Why My Life Sucks* list: a mental inventory of all the ways his life had nosedived since the new year. First on his list, chronologically, was having to move out of Grandad's house and into Kelch's apartment. Next came his mom making him go to a new school stuffed full of rich kids, where David got shoved and thumped daily for no reason he could ever figure out. Then the very worst thing: his grandfather died.

Since then, David had felt untethered. In the whole wide world, there was only one person left he felt connected to — his mother. David had a father too, of course, but only in the biological sense. Once David's mom had dug her heels in, insisted on finishing high school and decided to keep her baby, his father had bolted. He'd dropped out of school and headed west to work on the oil rigs, then disappeared. For David, that made it all the more important that he and his mother were a team. Since January, since moving into Kelch's apartment, his connection with his mother had felt . . . frayed. Especially now that she was so very angry with him about the fight.

When he closed his eyes, David saw that stack of boarding school brochures on Kelch's desk. His mother had said she wouldn't send him away, but Kelch always seemed to be able to talk her around to his way of thinking. The more David thought about that, the more he couldn't decide what would be worse — boarding school or going back to Rosehill Public School next Monday. At boarding school, he'd have nobody. He'd be completely alone. *But if I go back to Rosehill*, he thought, *I'm dead.*

It wouldn't be his backpack that got stuffed into the basket next time. It would be him.

He wiped his eyes with the back of his hand, went to his desk, grabbed the old jelly jar and tipped it over. There were no bills inside, just copper and silver. First, he slid them into piles of pennies, nickels, dimes and quarters. Then he counted them. Three dollars and twenty-seven cents. Twenty cents would buy him a children's fare ride on the subway to Union Station. From there, sixty-eight cents would get him a GO Train ticket as far west as Oakville or as far east as Pickering.

He was trying to decide if it was braver to stay or to run away when he heard the distinct creaking sound of someone climbing the stairs. He slid the money off his desk and funnelled it through his hands back into the jelly jar just as his mom walked into his room.

"You're supposed to knock," he said without thinking.

"Are you really going to sit there after being suspended from school for fighting and tell me what I'm supposed to do?"

David blanched.

"Well?" she said.

"Sorry."

She fished a pair of rubber boots out of his closet and dropped them on his desk. "Put these in your backpack and grab a jacket. We're going to take a look at the land your grandad left us. It's probably a bog or an overgrown jungle by now, and since you've only got one decent pair of sneakers . . ." She pointed at the rubber boots. When David didn't move, his mother asked, "Why are you just sitting there? Get your backpack."

"I don't have it anymore," he said.

"What do you mean you don't have it? Don't tell me you lost it?"

He shook his head.

She jammed her fists into her waist. Her lips were pressed together in a thin line. She looked fierce. "If you didn't lose it, where is it?"

David tried to swallow, but he couldn't. Like when he scooped peanut butter from the jar and ate it straight from the spoon, but this time it was words that got stuck in his throat. He didn't know what to do. If he told her about Marty, it would only remind her about school, the fight and the suspension. But the longer he took to answer the angrier she looked.

"It's stuck in the basketball net at school."

His mother looked confused.

"Marty stole my backpack with all my action figures and threw it into the basketball net."

"Why would he do that?"

"I dunno."

"There must be a reason, David. Did you say anything or do anything to him?"

David shook his head.

His mother's eyebrow's pinched together. "Are you sure?"

He nodded.

"Yesterday, you said Marty's been picking on you."

"Not just yesterday. Every day," David blurted, but somehow telling her made it worse. Like getting pushed around at school was his own fault. Kelch hadn't just moved into David's life, he'd moved inside his head too. Boys were supposed to be strong, Kelch would say, and strong boys don't get bullied.

His mother shook her head. "I wish you'd told me this before, David. Never mind. Here's what we'll do. Tomorrow I'll call your teacher and make sure she knows both sides of the story. I'll get them to look for your backpack too. With any luck, it will still be there."

David nodded. He didn't trust himself to speak yet.

"Violence is never the answer, David. You know that, don't you? What would your grandad have said?"

David dropped his head. "I'm sorry."

"What you did was wrong. But at least I understand why, and I *will* get to the bottom of what's been happening at school. You can take that to the bank." Then she smiled, and David felt like crying and laughing at the same time. His mother had barely looked at him since the school had called yesterday. Seeing her smile at him now was like seeing the sun rise. "In the meantime," she said, "I'll bring some plastic bags in case things are mucky on your grandfather's land. Now grab your boots, get ready and meet me downstairs. I'll wait by Cameron's car."

"What? Why is he coming?"

"Not this again, David."

"Why does he have to do everything with us? Why couldn't you have stayed with Larry, the guy who drove the city bus? He was fun. He used to take me to the arcade."

"Larry was a thirty-one-year-old man-child who lived in his parents' basement and had no plans to ever leave."

"We lived in Grandad's house."

"It's not the same, David."

David thought it was. "What about Wallace? He was great. He took us to the CNE, remember? Even Grandad liked him. He said Wallace was a hard worker."

His mom rolled her eyes. "Wallace worked hard in the summer so he could take off for six months to travel and write his novel. Wallace didn't want a family. Cameron does."

David shook his head. "He wants you, Mom. He doesn't want me. He doesn't even like me."

"If this is about yesterday in Cam's office, he was angry because you were screaming so loudly at him that his employees heard. You can understand why that upset him, can't you?" When David didn't answer, his mom said, "It's true, Cameron is a bit frustrated with you lately. He believes you need a firm hand."

"A firm hand across my butt," David muttered.

"Don't be ridiculous. Do you think I would let someone hit you? Well, would I?"

He shook his head.

It was true that Kelch had never raised a hand to him. But David thought he'd wanted to once or twice. And Kelch was always saying things like, "Stop that, David. You're like an annoying mosquito buzzing around my head." And everyone knew what you did to mosquitos.

"Cameron's quite a bit older than me, David," his mom said. "When he was growing up, people had old-fashioned ideas about children and how they should behave."

"Grandad was even older, but he wasn't like that. He never bossed me around. I could talk to Grandad about anything. He cared about me."

"Cameron does too."

"No, he doesn't!" David's chin quivered. "I see the way he looks at me."

"He just wants you to mind him."

"He wants me gone, Mom."

"Don't be silly."

"It's not silly. He said it! He wants to send me to boarding school. I saw those brochures on his desk, and I heard you guys talking about it in the living room last night. He wants to send me away so badly that he's willing to shell out a ton of money!"

His mother's eyes popped open wide as silver dollars, but she didn't deny it.

"Well, David," she said at last, "if you were eavesdropping, you will have also heard me tell him that I would never send you away." She walked to the door. "Now hurry up. Cameron is already outside. He's putting the convertible top down for the drive. Won't that be nice?"

As soon as she was gone, David picked up his jelly jar, poured all the coins into a sock, twisted the top as tightly as possible, then stuffed the coin-sock into his jeans pocket. He wasn't planning to run away — not yet anyway — but at least with those coins in his pocket, he felt like he had options. He slipped on a jacket, grabbed his rubber boots and headed out of his room. A green garbage bag sat on the floor in front of the door. David dropped his boots inside, then headed down the stairs. He stomped the whole way down, making those old steps groan and moan. They sounded exactly like he felt.

When he got to the small gravel parking lot, his mom was already sitting in the front seat. She wore her big Hollywood sunglasses and a white scarf, with the ends crossed under her chin, then tied in the back. She looked like a movie star from one of those old films his grandfather liked to watch.

"Hurry up, David," she called. "I'm dying to see this land your grandfather left us."

"Boots in the trunk," Kelch said. He leaned across the front seat and pushed the yellow button inside the glove box. The trunk popped open.

David mumbled, "I hate you," under his breath as he walked to the back of the car.

Once a week, Kelch had his Cadillac detailed, which, David had learned, was just a snooty word for a washed and vacuumed car. But even though Kelch kept the insides of the car looking brand new, the trunk — the part people couldn't see — was a mess. Kelch drove an expensive car, bragged about how much stuff he owned, but lived in a walk-up apartment above his office. Either he's a fake, David thought, or he's sitting on bags of money like a giant-sized Scrooge McDuck.

Soon they were on the highway. It was cold driving with the top down. David was glad he'd brought a jacket. His mom wore only a thin button-up sweater, and she looked cold. She had one hand on top of her head holding her scarf and the other wrapped around her body. David shrugged off his jacket and passed it forward. "Here, Mom," he yelled so she could hear him over the wind noise.

"What about you, David?"

"Nah, I'm fine."

"Thank you," she said with a BK smile.

BK. Before Kelch.

David leaned forward as far as the seatbelt would allow. With his chin almost resting on the front seat, he said, "What's the name of this place again, Mom?"

"Scotch Gully."

"Is that the name of the farm?"

"No. Scotch Gully is the town."

"But it's a farm, right? Grandad's place is a farm?"

"Once upon a time it was. Cameron called the

land registry office before we left and discovered that your grandfather's property has been in the Macrath family for a hundred years. Can you imagine, David? An entire century."

"And now?"

"Now? Well . . . we don't think it's a farm anymore."

"But it could be, right? There could be a barn and animals and stuff?"

"You watch too much television," Kelch said.

"What's TV got to do with it?" It was a smart-aleck remark but David couldn't help himself.

"You've got no idea what the real world is like," Kelch said. "You spend all your time reading comic books, watching happily-ever-after TV shows and playing make-believe with those dolls."

"They're action figures," David protested. "You wait, they'll be worth something someday."

"Cameron, David, please! Cameron, why don't you explain to David how you know the farm's been abandoned?"

Kelch patted her knee and nodded. "Fine. The public records say your grandfather inherited that land in 1948."

"That's before you were born, Mom."

"It is," she said. "And since I've lived in the Cabbagetown house ever since I was born—"

"In 1950."

"Yes, David. Since 1950. That means, realistically, it's been at least thirty years since anyone has lived on or farmed the land. Whatever it used to be, that farm will be overgrown and broken-down by now."

"But the land," Kelch said, grinning at my mom like a hungry hyena. "That land is what matters. It could be just the ticket."

Ticket for what? David should have asked then, but all he could think about was the possibility that maybe, just maybe, his luck was changing.

"Someone could be living there," David said.

"No." Kelch shook his head. "It's empty. Without a doubt."

He hoped Kelch was wrong. All the place would need was a house that was not too rundown. *Then Mom and I could move in*, David thought. He wouldn't have to see Kelch every day, and if they lived on a farm, there'd be enough room for a dog.

They'd left the city far behind when Kelch finally exited onto a much smaller highway. They were travelling slower now, but David's mom still had one hand on her scarf.

The scenery changed too. Everywhere David looked, there were fields and orchards, barns and tractors. They passed a turn-of-the-century church and one old farmhouse after another.

"I think we're close," Kelch said and slowed

down even more. "Check for numbers. Both of you. We're looking for three-eight-eight-zero."

David was the first to spot it. Mounted on top of a wooden post was a perfect miniature of a red barn with the numbers three-eight-eight-zero painted in black letters down the length of the post. Just then, a school bus pulled to a stop in front of the mailbox, blocking it from view. The bus's lights flashed, and a stop sign swung out from its side.

"Damn," Kelch muttered and stopped the car.

"It's right there, Mom. Behind that bus," David said. "That's three-eight-eight-zero."

"Can't be," Kelch said. "No one lives on your grandfather's land, and a school bus wouldn't stop where no one lived."

"But the mailbox said three-eight-eight-zero. I saw it."

Kelch shook his head. *He never listens to me*, David fumed. But at least once the bus pulled away, he would see David was right.

The school bus folded in its sign, and the flashers stopped, but Kelch didn't wait, didn't even bother to look. David twisted around to look out the back. He wanted to see who got off that bus. It was a girl about the same age as he was, walking up the driveway like she lived there.

"Forty-forty," David's mom called out a mailbox number.

David sank back in his seat and crossed his arms. *If he's not going to listen to me,* David thought, *I'm not going to bother looking.* At the next driveway and mailbox, his mom said, "Forty-two hundred. Cameron, we've passed it. Turn around."

"How did you miss it?" Kelch said. Grumbling, he turned the car around and headed back down the road.

"Stop!" David's mom squealed. "There it is, Cam. The one with the mailbox shaped like a red barn. Oh my God. That's so corny it's adorable."

"Told you so," David said.

Kelch shot David a look in the rearview mirror before heading up the drive at a crawl.

For a guy who was in such a hurry to get here, he's driving awfully slow, David thought. *I could walk faster than this.*

David forgot about how slowly Kelch was driving the second he saw his grandfather's farm. For the first time since his mom had dragged him away from his grandad's Cabbagetown house, from the only home he'd ever known, David felt a real surge of hope. This place wasn't old and broken down like Kelch said it would be. It was beautiful.

There was a farmhouse painted white with crisp red trim and red shutters. A huge veranda wrapped around the whole place. Way in the distance — behind and to the right of the farmhouse — there was a barn painted the opposite of the house. It had red boards with white trim. It was the real-life version of the mailbox out front. Far off to the left, there was an apple orchard. The trees were planted in straight lines, and still fluffy with white and pink blossoms. On the right was a fenced field dotted with a dozen or so fat sheep.

David undid his seat belt and leaned on the front seat to ask his mom a question. Tears rolled down her cheeks.

"Mom? What's the matter?"

"My father must have grown up here. Why didn't I know that? I wish . . ." She shook her head slowly side to side, leaving her sentence unfinished.

"But it's ours now, right?" David asked. He was making plans. He wanted a bedroom upstairs, so he could see far over the fields and trees.

His mom didn't answer. Instead, she put her hand on Kelch's arm. "Cam, do you see that?"

It was the girl from the bus.

"What are we going to do?" she asked.

"About her?" Kelch said.

She nodded.

"We do nothing. This place belongs to you, Carla. That child, whoever she is, is just a wrinkle. A wrinkle that I will iron out."

"I don't know, Cam. This place was supposed to be abandoned. But look at it."

"I am looking at it, Carla, and it's perfect." Kelch turned the engine off and took her hand. "Trust me, darling," he said. "Since the day I started Rosehill Realty, I've been scrimping and saving and working for an opportunity like this."

"But the girl," his mother said.

"She's unexpected, I admit. Maybe she's taking a shortcut through your land to her house. Don't worry. She won't be a problem. I promise."

Kelch leaned across the front seat and kissed David's mother. David almost gagged when she kissed him back. It was too much. He turned away and stared out the window.

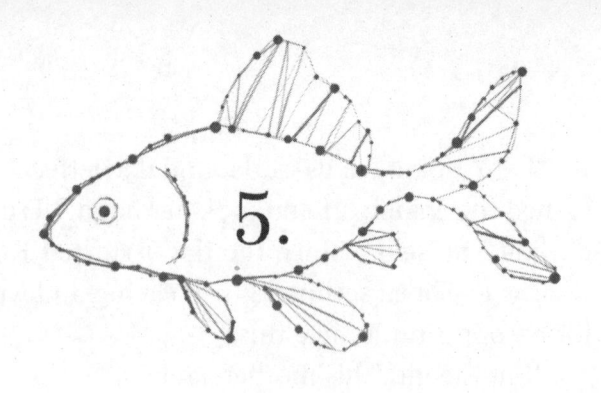

5.

Lizzie

I couldn't wait to ask Harry about the photograph I'd found yesterday, the one with the mysterious writing on the back. *Me and Archie Macrath. Graduation 1940.* My whole life, Harry had been talking about Mrs. Macrath's hairpins, Mrs. Macrath's coffee pots, Mrs. Macrath's *this*, and Mrs. Macrath's *that*. Never once had he bothered to mention that Mrs. Macrath had been a real person, and never once had I thought to ask. I figured Macrath was just a name like Kellogg, or Nestlé, or Hoover or John Deere. But now I'd seen a picture of a Macrath and learned that my grandma was friends with one of them, maybe more than friends, and I was curious. There had to be a good story there, and I wanted to hear it. I wondered if this was how my mom felt when she was a kid digging up that biscuit tin in the root cellar.

By the time the school bus dropped me off at the bottom of Harry's driveway, I felt all fizzy — like my muscles were full of Pop Rocks. As soon as my feet hit gravel, I started to run. I was almost at the porch steps before I spotted Harry. He was coming through the door, carrying our snack tray. Expo, the canine vacuum cleaner, was glued to his side, waiting for a taste. I could see a plate piled high with griddle cakes.

"Hey, boy," I hollered to Expo, but he ignored me. I never was as interesting to him as Harry's baking. Then, quick as a wink, Expo went stiff. His ears perked up, his head snapped over in my direction, and he started to bark.

People ears are no match for dog ears, so it took me longer to hear what Expo had heard — the growl of a large engine. When I turned to look, there, cruising up the drive at a crawl, was a big fancy convertible car.

"You expecting company, Harry?"

He shook his head.

"Do you know who it is?"

"Nope. I don't know anybody who would drive something like that. It looks like a Cadillac Eldorado."

"Must be just some city guy who got lost," I suggested.

"Must be."

I was surprised the car hadn't already done a turn-around and headed back to the road. Instead, it kept crawling forward. It was goofy how slow this guy was driving. I could run faster than that.

The car was still a good way back when the driver stopped and shut off the engine. The driver's-side door opened, and a man climbed out.

You can't tell much about a person from a distance. At least not the important stuff like are their eyes friendly and do they have smile wrinkles? But what I could see was that this guy was tall, really tall, and thin as a bulrush. I was about to ask Harry if he'd ever seen the man before when Expo growled. Maybe the growl was for the strange car, or maybe it was because Expo sensed something about the driver.

Harry had warned me that old dogs sometimes see threats when there aren't any. I hoped that wasn't what this was. I worried about what Harry would have to do if Expo went funny in his old age and bit someone. Around here, if a dog becomes a biter its owners are expected to put that dog down. I couldn't bear that. Expo was like family, and my family was already too small.

Expo let out a sharp warning bark, then fast as a blink he flew off the porch. I dropped my backpack and raced after him.

"Expo! Stop, boy!"

He wasn't listening. He was protecting the farm, barking like he did when a raccoon got in the hen-house.

At least he wasn't running right at the tall man anymore. Expo headed for the front of the car, running back and forth as if he could herd that big hunk of metal the same way he herded Harry's sheep.

Just when I was sure I'd make it, that I would reach Expo before anything bad could happen, a boy jumped out of the car. He didn't even bother to open the door. He climbed over it like he was a hockey player taking his shift on the ice. As soon as Expo saw the boy, he changed direction so fast his backside slid out to the left in a skid. I would have laughed at how cartoon-silly it looked if I wasn't so scared. As bad as things would be if Expo snapped at the tall man, they'd be a zillion times worse if he bit a kid.

Expo ran right at the boy, and the boy ran straight at Expo. In the space of a wing-flap, they met. Expo jumped up and slapped his paws on the boy's chest, almost knocking him over. By this point, I'd got myself so worked up about what could go wrong that I was close to tears. I went to pull Expo down when, miracle of miracles, I heard the boy laugh. It was music to my ears. Expo was licking the boy's face, and the boy liked it!

A lady appeared next, walking around the front

of the car. By this time, the boy was on his knees, his face buried in Expo's ruff, and Expo, big suck that he was, drank in the attention like it was a pail of freshly drawn well water on a hot day. Then the boy scratched Expo where he liked it best — along the seam between his ears and head. Anyone, even this fancy city lady, could see that they were getting along like old pals.

When the lady saw Expo and the boy, she smiled. She was pretty enough already, but when she smiled, she was beautiful.

"He's always wanted a dog," she said, then she slung her handbag over her shoulder and walked over to the raw-boned man. She leaned into his side, and he swallowed her in his arms.

Never in a million years would I have picked them as a family. The lady was young and curvy with movie-star looks; the man was way older and seemed to be made up of sharp angles from his nose to his knees. If you ask me, the boy didn't look much like his mom, and nothing at all like his dad.

Then without so much as an excuse me or a good afternoon, the man turned to me and asked, "Little girl, do you live here?"

Little girl? That raised my hackles, I can tell you. I was a teenager! I wanted to tell him so, let him know that I'd turned thirteen in March, but I minded my tongue. What I said instead was, "No, sir. I live down the road with my mom and grandma."

"But you are familiar with this place?"

I knew not to sass grown-ups, my grandmother made sure of that, but there was just something about this guy that was like a crusty scab — you know you're not supposed to pick at it, but you just can't help yourself.

"I'm here, aren't I?" I said, glad Grandma wasn't around to hear my smart mouth.

There was an uncomfortable stretch of quiet while we sized each other up. Then the man said, "I need to talk to whoever it is who seems to be in residence here."

Seems to be in residence, he said. That should have been my first clue, but I didn't notice.

"That would be Harry," I answered. "That's him over there."

I pointed to the porch. Harry was still standing in the shadows, holding the tray like we'd been playing frozen tag and he was waiting there for someone to unfreeze him. That should have been my second clue, but I missed that one too. Harry loves having visitors. It's usually just me, Mom, Grandma and the folks who buy Harry's eggs. Once every few months, the ladies from the Scotch Gully United Church Auxiliary, including Bethany Budge's gran, come here for a meeting. Old Mrs. Budge might want the villagers to pick up their pitchforks to run

Mom and me out of town, but she *adores* Harry. I've heard Grandma tell Harry that she thinks old Mrs. Budge is sweet on him.

The tall man headed toward the porch with the lady behind, scrambling to keep up with his long legs. That left me, the boy and Expo standing by the car. The boy had bright orange hair like my mom and a face that was more freckle than pink skin. Grandma liked to say freckles happened when you were kissed by an angel — one kiss equalled one freckle. If that were true, this kid had been smothered with more angel kisses than a fat baby at a christening.

I snorted at my own joke. I wanted to share it, but for no reason I could suss, the boy scowled at me then stomped off after his parents. Expo galumphed after him.

"Traitor," I muttered at Expo's backside, then scrambled to catch up.

On the porch, Harry put the snack tray down just as the man climbed the last step.

In a voice I could hear, even as far back as I was, the man said, "I'm Cameron Kelch, owner of Rosehill Realty."

Kelch. That's a disagreeable name. First off, Kelch rhymes with belch. Second, try saying it — the name sticks in the back of your throat like phlegm.

I felt sorry for the boy right then. It can't be nice

growing up with a last name like that.

Mr. Kelch didn't offer to shake Harry's hand. He just said, "And you are?"

"My name is Harry Doak."

"We need to have a conversation, Mr. Doak."

After what seemed like a forever-of-silence, Harry motioned for folks to sit down.

I tried to catch Harry's eye, but he was looking at the lady — Mrs. Kelch, I gathered — and smiling at her. It was a sad, faraway smile. Like when my mom looked at old black-and-white photos of Moonspinner, her horse.

I filed that thought away to mull over later because Mr. Kelch, the not-so-friendly giant, was pointing at the boy and saying, "This is an adult conversation. You kids go play."

When I didn't budge, he looked right at me and did that thing some grown-ups do where their mouths smile like they're your pal but their eyes look at you like you're the dirt they just stepped in.

"Go on. Off you go now."

At least he hadn't called me "little girl" again. I ignored him and looked at Harry.

"Harry?" I asked. "Do you want me to stay?"

He shook his head. "It's fine, Lizzie."

"Okay, then," I said, but I wasn't sure it was.

Harry turned to the boy. "Would you like to see the animals?"

"Yes!"

"I thought so. You could help Lizzie move the sheep from the pasture to the pen."

The boy nodded, a smile splitting his face.

"Help?" his dad snorted. Then he turned to the boy and said, "Behave yourself, and if you can't help, at least don't get in the way."

The boy's cheeks flushed bright pink and he looked down like he'd discovered something fascinating about his shoes. It can't be easy, I thought, having a father like that. Maybe it's not so awful that one half of my family tree was empty.

Harry asked, "Will you do that for me, Lizzie?"

"Sure, Harry," I answered.

But the look on my face must have given me away because he added, "This is a good thing. It will give you two a chance to get to know one another."

I couldn't for the life of me figure out why Harry thought it was such a swell idea for us to get to know one another, but I didn't ask. Or argue. Harry doesn't ask for much. And so with the biggest smile I could muster, I turned to the boy and said, "Come on, then. We'll go and see the ewes."

I started walking, but the boy stood rooted to the ground like a tree. I whistled for Expo. It was only when Expo ran after me that the boy made any move to follow. It didn't seem right to keep thinking of him as *the boy*, and I definitely couldn't call him that to his face, so when he caught up, I said, "I'm Lizzie. What's your name?"

"David," he mumbled.

I could not figure this kid out. It was almost like he was mad at me, but he couldn't be. All I'd done was smile at him since he arrived. Grandma says a smile is like a welcome handshake, but the bigger I smiled, the crankier this kid looked. I wondered if he'd had a dust-up with his dad on the way here and was still stuck in the fight. When Expo gets a cocklebur stuck in his coat, I have to distract him in order to pull it out. I decided to try that.

"Do you have a stomachache, David?" I asked.

He looked confused. Good.

"No?" It sounded more like a question than an answer.

"Sore throat? Headache?"

"No! I'm not sick."

"Then why does your face look like that?"

He stopped on a dime and glared at me. "Why were you laughing at me?"

"Huh? I wasn't laughing at you."

"Were too. Back at the car. You looked at me and laughed. Then you kept grinning like I was the punchline of some dumb joke."

There you go. It was a misunderstanding, is all. I pointed to my cheeks with both hands. "It's the freckles," I said.

"My freckles?"

I nodded, but that only seemed to make things worse. He got all swollen up and angry. "What about them?"

"When I saw you, it reminded me of something my grandma used to tell my mom. See, my mom has freckles just like you. Grandma would tell her that every one of her freckles was a kiss from an angel. When I remembered that, I pictured you being mobbed by a crowd of angels kissing you again and again and again. That's pretty funny, right?"

David made a face like he'd just stepped in dog poo. I'm not proud of it, but right then, I didn't feel like letting him help move the ewes. I wanted to give him a job to match his poo-sour face. I considered handing him a bucket and a pair of Harry's old rubber gloves, then sending him out into the pasture to collect ewe berries for manure tea. I couldn't do that, but I had an idea that was almost as good.

"Change of plan," I said. "Follow me, city boy."

He ignored me and crouched down, scratching Expo behind the ears. One look and I could see Expo was in doggy heaven. Somehow this crabby city kid had found Expo's happiness engine. This kid was hard work, no denying that. Still, I had never seen Expo take to anyone like he had to David, and the way I saw it, grumpy or not, anyone who got on this well with my dog couldn't be all bad.

Not all bad, but not good either. I was still prickled by how he was acting. A turn collecting eggs would serve him right. I made a beeline for the henhouse, whistling once again for Expo to follow. David might not like me, but I guessed he'd follow Expo anywhere. I did my best imitation of an Olympic speed walker, and sure enough, I could hear them both behind me hurrying to catch up.

"Where are we going? The sheep are that way," David said, pointing.

I pointed in the opposite direction, to a stand of maple trees way up ahead. Behind them, you could just see a tall wire fence. Inside the fence was a chicken-sized version of Harry's barn. "The henhouse," I said.

"That's a henhouse?"

"Yep. Harry made it a few years back. I helped him build and paint it."

"It looks like the mailbox out front," David said. He sounded impressed, and that kind of impressed me.

"You noticed?"

"Where I live, rich people have fancy kid playhouses in their backyards," he explained. "They look like that."

I figured this was just his way of bragging that he was rich. I'd already guessed that by the fancy car he'd rolled in on, but I didn't care if he was as rich as the Queen of England. Money didn't count with me. So with a voice sweeter than BeeHive corn syrup, I said, "Gosh, David, that's too bad."

"Too bad?"

"Yes. It's too bad that where you live, they make kids play in chicken coops."

I figured he'd growl at me for taking a poke like that, but right out of the blue, he started laughing like he was going to bust. Like his rich kid friends playing in chicken coops was some hilarious joke. I could not figure this one out at all, but his laugh was as contagious as a winter cold, and I started laughing too. Maybe I was wrong about him. Maybe he wasn't so bad after all?

At the henhouse, I reached for the basket that always hung on a peg on the fence.

"It's for the eggs," I said. "C'mon. But be careful when the gate opens not to let any of the girls out. Those rascals will run off and fly into the trees if they get a chance. Once they do, it's a pain to get them down."

"Chickens can't fly. Can they?"

"Not like robins or orioles, but they fly. Enough to get into a tree at least."

"Is that really true?"

"Cross my heart. And once they've made it onto a branch, they'll roost there all night if we let them."

He stared at me for a good few seconds more,

like he was trying to figure out if I was pulling his leg. Though why I'd lie about something as ordinary as chickens, I didn't know.

Finally, he said, "Why not let them stay in the trees if they like it?"

"Because the raccoons and owls would pick them off the branches and eat them."

"Oh," he said, wide-eyed, looking first at the chickens, then out at the trees. "I didn't know. I've got a lot to learn about farms, I guess. So how do you get them down?

"It's not easy. You've got to stun them all one by one."

David's eyes popped wide and his jaw dropped open. "You don't hit them, do you?"

"What?"

"To stun the chickens. You don't whack them over the head with a stick or something? Do you?"

A giggle threatened to bubble out my throat, but I bit the inside of my cheek until it went away. We were talking now, at least, and I didn't want to wreck that. If he thought I was laughing at him, he might clam up again. With as much seriousness as I could muster, I said, "You wait until dark, then shine a flashlight in their eyes. That stuns them enough so you can grab them and put them back inside the coop."

David chewed the corner of his bottom lip like

he was thinking hard. But the chickens spotted me and started to squawk. I reached for the gate.

"Wait, Lizzie."

"What is it?"

"Sorry I snapped at you before. I only did it because I thought you were making fun of me and, well, I get enough of that from the kids at school."

"You mean all your rich friends who play in henhouses?"

He snorted. "Yeah, them. But they're not my friends. Friends don't shove you around, steal your stuff and call you names."

"No, they don't," I agreed, thinking of Bethany Budge. I didn't ever want to be that hateful. So when David held up his index and middle fingers in the V-sign and said, "Peace?" I smiled and flashed the peace sign right back at him. But I felt rotten. I'd decided to make David collect eggs because he'd been such a pain in the butt. Now that we were friendly, it felt mean.

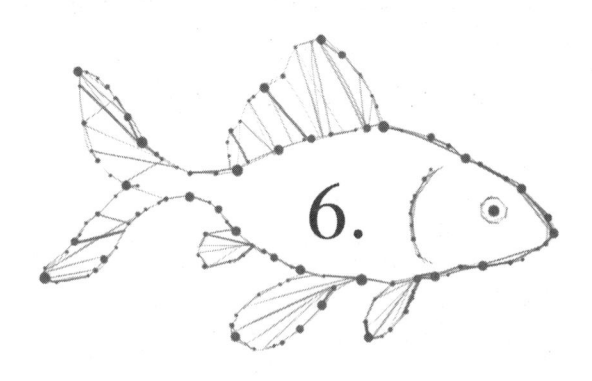

6.

Darvid

There were chickens everywhere. Some waddled up and down the ramp to the henhouse door. Even more milled about inside the coop fence, pecking on the dirt. Some were white, some were black and some, David noticed, were the same red-brown colour of the Irish setter he'd dreamed of getting and naming Archie, for his grandfather.

After the epically rotten twenty-four hours he had just spent in solitary, David could hardly believe he was actually here, on the same farm where his grandfather had lived as a boy. Maybe things really were getting better. Grinning, David turned to ask Lizzie a question about collecting eggs. He could tell right away something was wrong. Lizzie was gnawing at the corner of her bottom lip. She wore the same pinched-together eyebrows and forehead wrinkles his grandad used to get when he was worried about something. She even looked a bit like him, David thought.

"Lizzie, is everything okay? Can we go inside now?" David knew he'd been a grump earlier, but he hoped they'd gotten past that.

Lizzie continued to chew her lip, then she took a deep breath, turned to David and said, "Let's go." She pulled the gate open a sliver. Expo made a lunge for the gap, but Lizzie was quicker and shot her leg across the opening, blocking his way. With her free hand, she pushed David inside, then slid in after him. She'd barely got the gate closed before the brood of hens started toward them, with Expo on the outside barking.

"Go back to Harry," Lizzie said to the dog. When Expo didn't move, she said, "Harry's got griddle cakes."

As if a dog would understand that, David thought, but sure enough, Expo turned around and padded off toward the farmhouse. David watched in awe, convinced more than ever that dogs make life better.

"Expo loves chasing chickens," Lizzie said. "He'd never hurt the girls, but he gets them so worked up they stop laying for a few days. Look out! Here they come."

Moments later, David was surrounded by noise and feathers. Lizzie tried to tell him the who's who of hens, but David could barely hear her over the squawking.

"There's Alice, Queenie, Nugget, Miss Piggy—"

"You have a chicken named Miss Piggy?" David asked.

"Wait. You'll see why."

David watched as Lizzie pried the lid off a large white plastic pail with *scratch* written on the outside in permanent marker.

"Go ahead," she told him. "Scoop's inside."

As he reached into the pail, the chickens crowded around his legs, squawking *chook chook chook* and pecking.

"Shoo," Lizzie cried, bending over and swinging her arms. "Hurry up, David."

David filled the scooper and looked around. "Where do I put it?" he called back over the noise. "Is there a bowl or something?"

"Chickens aren't like dogs. Just sprinkle it on the ground. Like this." She gestured how to do it, but the chickens didn't know Lizzie's hand was empty and they raced around in circles looking for the food she'd only pretended to throw. David laughed.

"Chickens need to eat off the ground," she called over the noise. "It's for their digestion. Uh-oh. They're coming back. Go on, David. Do it. Do it now!"

David threw the entire scoop, broadcasting it all

over the ground. Like a school of fish, the chickens turned as one and ran for their dinner. One reddish-brown chicken pushed her way through the flock to the front. She was loud and fat with a collar of white feathers around her neck.

"Miss Piggy?" David asked.

"Yep," Lizzie said chuckling. "She's so pushy. See the way she struts?"

"I get it now." He smiled. "That ring of white feathers is like Miss Piggy's pearl necklace."

"Exactly! She's a real pest, that one."

With the chickens busy eating, it was a lot quieter in the yard. David asked, "What was that stuff in the pail that I fed them?"

"Scratch? It's a mix of seeds, corn and cereal."

"So it's kind of like granola for chickens."

"Ha! Good one, David."

David grinned a smile so wide his cheeks pinched. *This must be what it's like to have a friend,* he thought.

Lizzie pointed to a chicken that was lagging behind the rest. "See the one with the funny eye and no upper beak? That's Alice. A raccoon got in last year and killed three of the hens. We almost lost Alice too, but Harry nursed her back to health."

"Is she going to be okay?" David asked.

"She'll live, but she hasn't laid an egg since the attack. We usually don't keep a hen unless she's laying, but Harry said we have to make an exception for Alice because she's been through the wars."

"That's a funny saying."

"Been through the wars? I think it's British. Like Harry."

"Harry didn't sound British."

"That's because he's been here a long time. He got sent here when he was a little kid. Harry was a British home child."

David didn't know what that was, but he didn't want Lizzie to think he was dumb, especially not now that they were getting along so well. He nodded and changed the subject.

"Is this all chickens eat?" he asked. "Scratch?"

"No. We give them vegetable peelings too. It makes their yolks brighter yellow. People around here like that. And in the winter, Harry sprinkles a little sand and small gravel on the run."

"So they don't slip and fall," David said, nodding. "We do the same thing to sidewalks in the city."

"No. Not for that, silly. The chickens eat it."

"They eat gravel?" David wasn't sure if he'd heard her wrong. Was this a gag, or was it another strange farm fact like chickens being able to fly?

Lizzie explained. "Chickens don't have teeth. They need sand and stones in their gizzards to break up their food. In the winter, they can't always peck through the snow and ice to the dirt below, so—"

"I sure have a lot to learn," David said. "I should probably get a notebook and write this stuff down. Can we collect the eggs now?"

Lizzie's eyebrows pinched together again in that familiar way that reminded David of his grandfather. David worried that she'd changed her mind about collecting the eggs. Worse, what if she'd changed her mind about him? He really hoped that wasn't true. Once he and his mother moved here, David was already counting on having Lizzie around. She was nice and funny, everything a friend should be. But there was another reason — a selfish reason. Lizzie knew all about the farm and its animals. She'd be able to help him learn about becoming a farmer.

She headed up the ramp to the henhouse. David scrambled after her.

It was dark inside, and it smelled. It reminded David of the ammonia cleaner his grandfather used to use. When his eyes adjusted to the dark, he noticed the henhouse floor was covered in a thick layer of straw.

"How do you find the eggs without stepping on them?" he asked. He imagined dozens of chicken eggs buried under the straw, invisible. Like the foil-wrapped chocolate eggs his mother would hide each year beneath a mound of green plastic Easter grass.

"That's what the nesting boxes are for." Lizzie pointed to two rows of five boxes fastened to the far wall, one on top of the other. "They lay their eggs in there."

David peered inside the first box. There were two eggs — one white, one brown. He started to reach in, but Lizzie grabbed his arm and held him back.

"Wait, David." There it was again, that funny look, all pinched and grumpy. "Let me do it," she said.

David pulled his arm free. He didn't know why Lizzie had changed her mind about him, but he really wanted to do this. The farm was going to be his life now — living here in the house his grandfather grew up in, collecting fresh eggs every day, then cooking and eating them at the same kitchen table where his grandfather would have sat at David's age. After yesterday, this was a better life than he could have dared dream.

"I'll be careful, Lizzie." And before she could stop him, David reached in and picked up an egg. It didn't look like an egg from the grocery store. It didn't feel like one either. It wasn't as smooth.

"I think there's something wrong with this one," he said.

"There's nothing wrong with the egg, David. Here, put it in the basket. I'll get the rest."

"Wait a sec. How come it looks like that? Is it from a special kind of hen?" David had never seen a live chicken before, but he still knew the basics; brown chickens laid brown eggs, and white chickens laid white eggs. That was *Sesame Street*–type knowledge. This was a white chicken egg, but it was covered with messy brown spots and streaks.

Lizzie stuck out her hand. "Give it to me."

"How come? What did I do wrong?"

"You didn't do anything wrong. It's just—"

"Just what?"

"That egg you're holding is covered in chicken poop. Hand it over. I'll finish up."

Yuck. David's dream of farm egg breakfasts didn't seem so appealing anymore, but still he hung on to the egg.

"Just let me do it, David. It doesn't bother me. I do this every day."

David's face knotted up. "You knew this was going to happen, didn't you? That I'd get an egg covered in chicken poop?"

Lizzie looked down at her shoes and nodded. "Since the raccoon got in last year, there are almost always a few dirty eggs."

"You mean the time that Alice lost her beak?"

"Yeah. It's probably Alice messing on the eggs. Harry thinks she started sleeping in the nesting boxes after the attack because it makes her feel safer."

David understood wanting to feel safe.

"But, David, even when the boxes are clean and no one's sleeping inside, there's still no guarantee. Chickens poop out of the same vent they lay their eggs from."

"So how come you wanted me to pick up pooped-on eggs?" he asked.

Lizzie shrugged her shoulders right up to her ears and held them there for so long David didn't think she was ever going to answer. Finally, she said, "You were such a grump at first. I thought you were sticking your nose up at Harry's farm. That made me angry. I love this place and, I dunno, I guess I figured this might be a funny way to teach you a lesson. But I'm sorry, David. Really."

David had been apologized to by fakers. Even Marty had apologized once. "Sorry," he'd said right before he shoved David in the chest so hard that he fell on his butt. Marty had walked away, laughed, and then called back, "Sorry, for not being sorry."

Lizzie wasn't faking. David could hear it in her voice and see it on her face. Everything about her said that she really, truly, hand-over-heart felt bad. *And she did try to stop me from picking up that egg,* he thought.

"By the time I saw that you were different, that I liked you," Lizzie said, "we were already here. I didn't know what to do."

"You could have just told me."

"I wanted to, but I thought if I did, you might not want to . . . I dunno, become friends?" She shrugged her shoulders up again.

Friends. She'd said it. We could be friends.

David gave her a gentle shoulder check. "It's okay, Lizzie," he said. "And don't worry. I've got this." Then he turned back to the nesting boxes, checked each box one by one, and gently placed every egg he found into the basket. When he was finished checking all ten boxes, he had thirty-five eggs, and even though he'd touched chicken poop, this was by far the coolest thing he'd ever done.

"That's all of them," he said, standing tall. Lizzie grinned at him, and he stood even taller. Then it dawned on him; this was a lot of eggs for one old man. "Hey, Lizzie," he asked. "What's Harry going to do with thirty-five eggs?"

"He sells them. He's got standing orders for every day of the week plus a waiting list of people in case he gets extras or someone cancels. Everybody wants fresh eggs."

Harry. Sells. Eggs.

David's hand moved to the lump of coins in his pocket. In the city, it had taken him months to save three dollars and twenty-seven cents. *But this farm is ours now*, he thought, *mine and Mom's*. With thirty-five eggs every day — David scrunched his eyes and pictured doing the math on paper. Seven days a week, multiplied by thirty-five eggs, that's . . . that's two hundred and forty-five eggs to sell every week! Maybe if he did all the work, his mom would let him keep the money.

Lizzie headed down the henhouse ramp and across the coop to the fence. David followed close behind, being extra careful with the basket. The chickens saw him and came running at his legs, clucking and squawking.

"Are they mad because I'm taking their eggs?" he called over the noise.

Lizzie was Lizzie again. She laughed. "No. They're just greedy. They think you're going to give them more scratch. Hang on. I'll shift them." She swung her arms wide and called, "*Shoo shoo.*"

David moved quickly into the space she'd made, careful not to jostle the eggs.

Lizzie did one last big arm waggle, followed by a loud holler, and the chickens scattered enough that David could squeeze through the gate to the outside. Lizzie followed quickly, latching it behind them.

"Follow me," she said.

"Where are we going?"

"To the house. We've got to wash the eggs, but I'll tell you about the farm on the way and you can pick what you want to see next."

David already knew what he wanted to see. Expo and that barn. He looked around for the dog, but Expo was nowhere to be seen. Lizzie was already walking to the farmhouse. David followed her, falling a few steps behind. It wasn't easy to walk quickly while carrying a basket full of eggs and trying not to break any.

"C'mon, slowpoke," Lizzie said. "You can go faster than that. You're carrying eggs, not walking on eggshells."

"Har-de-har-har," David said, catching up. His stomach growled. Lizzie heard it and laughed. "Your stomach is in luck. I saw Harry with a plate of griddle cakes earlier."

"Griddle cakes?"

"You've never had one? Oh, man, you're going to love them. They're soooo good."

"Are they like pancakes?"

"More like mini-scones."

David shook his head. He'd never had those either. His mom wasn't much of a baker. She was more of a buy-the-broken-cookies-by-the-pound kind of mom.

"Just wait until you try one. Mmmm-mmm delicious," Lizzie said, rubbing a hand over her stomach. "Don't ever tell my grandma I said this, but Harry is the best baker in all of Scotch Gully."

"Harry bakes?" David asked. "But he's a man."

Lizzie giggled. "Mom says Harry is the perfect modern man. He farms, fixes tractors, makes furniture, cooks, bakes and babysits. He's been babysitting me since I was born. And my mom before that. She started coming to Harry's after school when she was in kindergarten. This place is our second home. And Harry . . . well, we're not blood relatives, but he's family."

David had that roller-coaster feeling again. He'd been so excited about moving here with his mother that he hadn't thought about anyone else. Now he understood that when they moved in, it meant that Harry would have to move out. David didn't know Harry — he was just the old guy he'd seen standing on the porch when they drove up. But Lizzie knew him, and it sounded like she loved him. Maybe even as much as he'd loved his grandad.

David gripped the egg basket tighter.

"Lizzie?"

"What is it?"

He was almost afraid to ask.

"If Harry babysat your mom, he must have lived at the farm a long time?"

"Ages. He came here right after the war. He doesn't talk about it much, but I know that he was in the 3rd Canadian Infantry Division. You know, the one that landed at Juno Beach. Harry was a hero."

David felt goosebumps rise up and down both

arms. His grandad was in the 3rd Canadian Infantry Division too. One of David's favourite stories was about his grandad at Juno Beach. The Germans had men defending Juno, and when the Allied forces landed, the Germans started shooting. Everyone scattered, running for cover. Some ran right into German land mines buried in the sand. His grandfather had hurt his knee jumping onto the beach and thought he was a goner until he looked up and saw his best friend running back for him, dodging bullets, land mines and dead soldiers to drag him to safety.

For a second, David could hardly breathe. Could Harry be the friend who saved his grandfather's life? Nah, couldn't be. He shook his head and pushed that crazy thought far away. Lizzie was talking again.

"Sorry, Lizzie. What did you say?"

"Remember when I told you that Harry was a British home child?"

"Sort of. But I don't really know what that is."

"That's okay, David. Most people don't. I probably wouldn't have known about them either if it weren't for Harry. Harry was born in England. When he was four, he got put in a home."

"Like an orphanage?"

"Sort of. Except most of the kids in those homes weren't orphans. Some higher-ups thought there were too many poor kids begging on the streets in England, so they dreamed up a plan. They rounded up poor kids and kids with only one parent and put them all into children's homes."

Lizzie's eyes narrowed then, and her face became stormy. She drummed her pointer finger hard against her own chest. "I've only got one parent," she said. "My dad took off as soon as he learned my mom was pregnant. If I'd lived in England back then, maybe they'd have taken me away."

David saw how difficult that was for Lizzie to say, and because they were becoming friends — she'd said so — and because he trusted her now, he shared his own story, something he'd never done before. "They might have taken me too, Lizzie. My mom's never been married. Grandad said she was smart not to hitch herself to a broken wagon."

Lizzie snorted. "That sounds *exactly* like something my grandma would say." Then her eyebrows pinched together again. "So who's that guy with your mom? Your stepfather?"

"Kelch? No!" David shook his head. He didn't even want to think about what his life would be like if his mom and Kelch got married. "Kelch is my mom's boyfriend. We live with him. That's all." But David didn't want to talk about Kelch. He wanted to figure out if Harry was the guy who'd saved his grandfather's life. If he was, that changed things.

"How long was Harry in that orphanage place?"

"Not long. As soon as Harry turned five, he was loaded onto a ship with a bunch of other British home children and sent to Canada. Can you imagine what that was like for them?" Lizzie asked.

David shook his head. "He was adopted by a nice family when he got here, right?"

Lizzie shook her head. "Nope. He was sent to work on a farm in Saskatchewan."

"That's nuts, Lizzie. A five-year-old can't work."

"I know. It's nuts, right? But he had to work, even though he was the youngest one there."

"There were more?"

"There were about a dozen British home children working at the farm. They were all indentured."

"Hold on, what's indentured?" David thought it sounded like dentures, but he couldn't figure out how kids and false teeth went together.

They'd reached the farmhouse. Lizzie sat on the top step and David sat down beside her. From the back porch steps he could see the chicken coop and barn to the right. To the left was a large L-shaped patch of freshly turned dirt. It looked like Harry was getting ready to plant a garden. David's grandad had a garden.

"Indentured means they had to work. All the British home children were indentured."

"How come you know so much about this stuff?"

"Oh, 4-H Club. Around here 4-H is mostly about farming, but our club also does speeches and my mom thought it would be good for me. I had to pick a topic—"

"British home children?"

"Yep. Then do research—"

"Talking to Harry?"

"Right again. Then I had to give a speech about it. I *really* don't like public speaking."

"Me neither," David said. "So Harry told you what it was like?"

"He said if they didn't like him, or they were finished with him, they could send him back or trade him for another kid."

Kelch would trade me in a heartbeat if he could, David thought. He shook off that thought and focused on finding out more about Harry.

Lizzie continued. "Harry says they never got enough to eat at the farm, and if they didn't work hard enough, or if they asked for more food or extra blankets, the farmer would beat them."

Kelch had never hurt David. But it hadn't escaped David's attention that when he refused to do what he said, Kelch became all tight. His neck got veiny and he would ball his fists over and over like he wanted to hit something. Or someone.

"I hate how mean some people can be," Lizzie said.

Me too, thought David. "So how did Harry end up here?"

"When he was older, he ran away from the farm. He headed east, getting work when he could, but basically, he lived on the street. It was rough. By the time he got to Toronto, he had no money, no food and no clothes save the ones on his back. He figured it was all over for him, and that he'd soon die of hunger or cold."

David's hand reached for the sock of coins in his pocket. Running away seemed a lot scarier to David now. But Lizzie had said that Harry was a hero and David wanted to hear why. Could it be because of something that happened on D-Day at Juno Beach?

"So then what happened?" he asked.

"Harry joined the army and was sent overseas."

"That's how he ended up on Juno Beach."

"Yep. Harry pulled someone from the beach. If it wasn't for Harry, that guy would have died."

David clutched the basket of eggs tighter, hugging it to his chest. The hairs on his arms stood on end. Even his goosebumps had goosebumps.

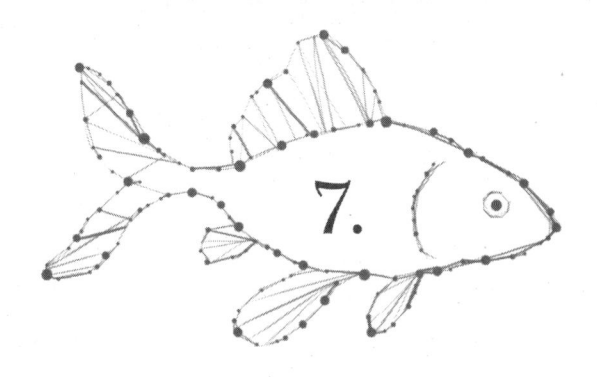

7.

Lizzie

Something was wrong, I could tell. David and I had been talking, easy and comfortable like old friends. The whole time he'd been all "Har-de-har-har," and chock-full of questions and then, quick as a tick, he started to white-knuckle that basket of eggs he was carrying.

"Spit," I said. "What's wrong?"

He chewed his bottom lip. "Lizzie, I've got to tell you something."

"Okay."

"I don't know where to start."

"How about you think about it while we go inside and wash the eggs. You better wash your hands too because . . . you know . . . chicken poo."

I stood up, and as I pulled open the screen door, Expo came running down the porch. I swear that dog has a sixth sense about getting into the kitchen.

"Hey, boy," David said, giving Expo a good scratch behind the ears. And just like that, David was all smiles again. Just the sight of Expo had turned him from hangdog to happy-puppy. David wasn't bothered that my dog's belly and legs were a soppy brown mess. But I knew after one look at Expo's muddy self that once company left, Harry and I would be dragging out Mrs. Macrath's blue-and-white enamel tub to give him a bath.

"He's been down at the creek again," I told David. "Probably chasing rabbits." To Expo, I said, "Go on, boy. Away you go." Then I opened the kitchen door.

It was like the chicken coop all over again. Expo headed for the open door when he knew full well he wouldn't be allowed in. Before he could slip past me into the kitchen, I grabbed him. "Oh no, you don't, Mr. Muddy Paws."

I nodded for David to go inside. Expo whined; he knew the kitchen held treats. Once David was on the other side of the screen door, I let go. Expo took a few steps away, did a full body shake that sent mud and water flying everywhere, then padded away along the porch toward Harry and his guests.

"Stinker," I muttered. David laughed.

Inside the kitchen, I reached under the sink for the empty ice cream pail and the green scouring pad we use to wash the eggs. Folks here want their eggs fresh, but they want them clean too. I squirted dish soap into the bucket, filled it with warm water, folded a clean dishcloth and set it on the counter beside the sink. With Expo gone, David looked out of sorts again. I touched my pointer finger to the tip of his nose. His eyes popped wide open.

"There you are," I said.

I didn't know what had David so tied up in knots or why he couldn't talk about it, but I did know one thing for certain.

"I like you, David," I told him. "You're a goldfish."

"Huh?"

His eyes went so wide he looked like a flashlight-stunned chicken stuck up a tree. I couldn't help giggling.

David's forehead puckered. "Because goldfish are orange? Like my hair?" he asked.

"No, silly. Being a goldfish has nothing to do with how you *look*. It's about *this*," I said, touching a finger to his chest. "It's about *how* you are. It's about heart."

David looked down at my hand, then he shook his head. "I don't get it. Do you think I'm dumb?"

"No! Of course not. Why would you say that?"

"Because goldfish are dumb. They just swim around in a bowl all day, bumping their noses on the glass, waiting for someone to feed them. They're clueless. Wait. Do you think I'm a goldfish because I'm clueless about farm stuff?"

"No, goofball. It's not about that. It's about what goldfish can become. What happens if you take a tiny goldfish outside and dump it into a pond?"

"I dunno. It dies?"

"It doesn't die. That's the whole point. If you dump a goldfish straight from a bowl into a pond, it will grow and grow and grow. A goldfish this size," I said, holding up a pinky finger, "can grow to be a foot long or more if the pond is big enough and deep enough."

"I still don't get it," he said.

"This is your pond," I said. "This farm. You've only been here a short while and look at what you've done already. Imagine what you could do if you spent more time here."

"Like a goldfish," he said, nodding.

I gave him a soft shoulder check like the one he'd given me earlier, and he gave me back a smile. Then I had a brilliant idea.

"Hey, David, why *don't* you spend more time here? Would your mom let you come this weekend? The lambing is about to start any day now. If you thought the chickens were neat, wait until you see a lamb being born. I get to name the first one." I told him the names I'd chosen for a ewe lamb, and David burst out laughing. Finally. Somebody gets me.

"What do you say? Do you want to come this weekend?" I asked. "If it stays nice we could even sleep in the hayloft in the barn."

David wore a grin that stretched ear to ear, but it lasted for only a second before his face clouded over again. I wished he would just spit out what was bugging him.

"Here," I said. "Give me those." I peeled his fingers from the egg basket, then turned to the sink and placed the eggs one by one in the bucket of soapy water.

"You wash," I said.

David stepped up to the sink like a sleepwalker. I showed him how to wash an egg and set it gently on the dishcloth to dry. While David washed the rest of the eggs, I fetched the empty cartons from the top of the fridge. Then I pulled open Harry's junk drawer. Inside was a jumble of string, elastics, twist ties, a pair of scissors, a measuring tape, a mess of pens and pencils, and a wad of wonky notepaper squares that Harry had cut from the backs of used envelopes and old circulars. Underneath all that, I found what I was looking for — a marking pen. I reached for one of the washed eggs. I chose a dry one, wrote across it, then added eleven more eggs to the carton. On the closed lid, in great big letters, I wrote DAVID.

"These are for you to take home," I said. "My

phone number's on one of the eggs. Call me, okay? After we talk to our moms about this weekend."

David didn't answer. He just chewed hard on his lip like he was fighting a war with himself.

"Spit," I demanded.

Finally, he took a deep breath and said, "I think my grandad and Harry knew each other."

"That's what has you in such a muddle?"

It seemed a silly thing to be worried about. I asked, "Why do you think that? Because they were both in the 3rd Canadian Infantry Division?"

He nodded again. "That's part of it."

"That would be neat if it were true. But, David, aren't there are thousands of men in a division? The chances that your grandad and Harry ever met have to be pretty small, right?"

He started chewing his lip again. Before he chewed right through to the gristle, I said, "Why don't you ask your grandad when you get home?"

"I can't." David dropped his head. "He died a few weeks ago."

Around here, when someone dies, people say, "I'm sorry for your loss." But that was like saying "God bless you" automatically when someone sneezes. It wasn't enough. David needed a hug. I almost did it too, but we hadn't been friends for more than a minute, and I worried it might seem weird.

"Sometimes I pick up the phone to call him and

then remember he's gone," David said. "I miss him like crazy. He was my best friend. It still hurts like a punch in the gut."

It's hard to watch anybody hurting, but seeing David hurt was extra hard. I knew it didn't make sense — we'd just met, plus we'd started off all vinegar and baking soda — but I really liked David. It wasn't only because he took to Harry's farm like a duck to water. There was something comfortable about him. Familiar. At first, I figured it was because, with his freckles and orange-red hair, he looked so much like my mom. But deep down, it felt like something else. Like we were connected somehow. So even though I really, *really* wanted to do something to make him feel better, I just stood there like a dope.

"Lizzie, what if it was Harry who saved Grandad's life on Juno Beach? If that's true, then . . ."

"Then that's great!" I said and meant it, but David went back to chewing his lip. "Don't you see, David? We'd be like family then. Not blood relatives or anything, but still . . ." My words trailed off as my brain worked double time, imagining how great that would be. Maybe *not* blood relatives, but close enough.

David shook his head.

"What the matter with you? This is good news."

"Lizzie, do you know what a will is?"

"My mom's a lawyer, so yeah."

"So . . . the thing is . . ." David took a deep breath then spit out the next sentence so fast that I didn't understand him. "*Mygrandadleftusthisfarminhiswill.*"

"What? Say it slower."

"My grandad left us this farm in his will."

"Which farm?"

"This one."

It's a good thing I'd finished putting all the clean eggs in their cartons because, for sure, I would have either dropped one or squashed it to bits in my fist.

"My grandad inherited the farm from his parents," David said. "And my mom got it when Grandad died."

"No." I shook my head. "You're wrong. Harry came here soon after the war ended, and my mom's been coming to Harry's after school from the very beginning. Ever since she started kindergarten." To prove my point, I explained, "My mom was born April 1st, 1941, and kids are five years old when they start kindergarten, so that means she started coming here to be cared for by Harry in 1946. See? This is Harry's place. It's always been Harry's."

"I can't figure that part out," David said. "But maybe it's because of what you told me about Harry being a British . . . what did you call it?"

"British home child."

"Yeah. That. Harry had no family, right?"

"What's that got to do with the price of tea in China?" I asked, angry.

"If Harry was the one who saved my grandad's life on D-Day, and he had no family and no place to go after the war, then my grandad letting Harry stay here might have been a thank you. That makes sense, right?"

I shook my head. Nothing made sense. Hearing this farm wasn't Harry's turned my world upside down. I told myself it couldn't be true. It just couldn't.

"Don't be mad, Lizzie. Please!" David said. "We didn't think anyone lived here. We thought the place was abandoned."

"Well, it's not abandoned, is it?" I was almost yelling, and that was not something I did. I hated arguing. It tied my stomach up in knots. I was so upset I was afraid that if I tried to say any more, I'd bawl.

"I've got to talk to Harry," I said. I needed to hear him tell me this was all one giant mistake.

I left David standing in the kitchen and ran to the front porch. I got there just in time to hear Kelch say, "The bottom line, Mr. Doak, is that this farm does not belong to you. You need to make whatever arrangements necessary for your future because we will need you to move out by July 1st."

"No!" I cried. "You can't do that."

I felt a hand slip into mine. It was David. He'd followed me.

"Lizzie's right, Mom," David said. "You can't kick Harry out." Then David turned to Harry. "It is you, isn't it? You're Grandad's best friend. You saved his life on Juno Beach."

My heart thumped a million times a minute. I watched, hardly able to catch my breath as Harry nodded, tears in his eyes. "You look just like him, David. Seeing you is like seeing Archie. It does my heart good."

"Archie?" I croaked. I looked from David to Harry and back to David again. I had never felt so muddled in all my life.

"Archie Macrath," David explained. "My grandad."

Macrath? Like the writing on the back of Grandma's photo.

Me and Archie Macrath. Graduation 1940.

Right then and there, I came unstuck. My world shattered into a billion pieces, and I didn't think there was enough glue in existence to put things back together, the way they should be.

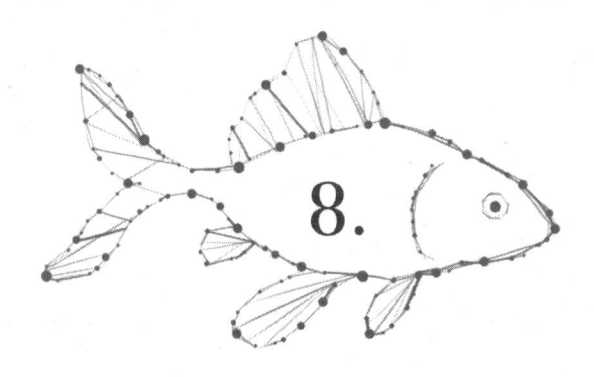

David

David caught up with Lizzie just as Kelch broke the news: Harry had to leave the farm by July 1st. It hurt David to see how small and scared Lizzie looked right then. It was as if all of the brightness had leaked out of her heart and evaporated. David wished there was time to take her aside and talk, but he had to make things right first. He had to make his mother understand who Harry was and why it would be wrong to make him leave. David reached for Lizzie's hand and squeezed it gently, hoping she would realize he was on her side.

He turned to his mother and said, "Harry was the one who saved Grandad's life on Juno Beach, Mom. If it wasn't for Harry, you wouldn't have been born. Me neither. So, you see, you can't kick him out."

"David?"

"Don't you get it, Mom? Harry being here was Grandad's idea. That's right, isn't it, Harry?"

Harry smiled warmly at David, a genuine smile that shone through his eyes, then he nodded. Kelch snorted and started to stand, but David's mother put her hand on his knee and said, "Cam, please." To Harry, she said, "How did you come to be living here, Mr. Doak? I'd like to hear that story."

Harry nodded, then began. "I was a Barnardo boy, a British home child, sent over from England to work on a farm. It was no life for a child, but I had nowhere else to go, and I was so young. Years later, when I was old enough and brave enough, I ran away. By June 1940, I'd worked my way from Saskatchewan to Toronto, but by then I had no money, no food and no clothes except the ones on my back. I tried to get work, but no one would hire me, the state I was in.

"This country had recently declared war on Germany. Our boys were going overseas to fight Hitler, and I reasoned that if I joined the army, they would give me boots, clothes, a winter coat and three square meals a day. Not the noblest reason for joining the army, but there you are. I was hungry and desperate. I made my way to a recruiting office, and there, standing in line — in those days, there were long lines of young men eager to serve — I met Archie. He'd hitchhiked to the city to join the war.

"He had such a big heart, Archie. He was waiting his turn to enlist when he saw the army reject me. Right then and there, he stepped out of line and offered to help. He bought me a hot meal and gave me a change of clothes. He even paid for a room at the YMCA, where I had my first-ever hot shower. I can tell you, I thought that was heaven. Hot water and indoors too." Harry shook his head before he continued. "Well, the next day, Archie and I returned to the recruiters, and this time they accepted me. That's what I meant when I said that Archie saved my life. I doubt I would have survived another winter living rough in Toronto."

"Then what happened?" David asked, hungry for stories about his grandfather.

"Both of us were placed in the 3rd Canadian Infantry Division. Eventually, we landed in England. We didn't know it at the time, but we were being readied for the D-Day invasion of Normandy. Our target was Juno Beach."

David turned to his mother. "Grandad always said that if it wasn't for his best friend pulling him to safety, he would have died on that beach in France. Remember, Mom?"

His mother started to speak, but Kelch placed a hand across her arm to stop her, which angered David. *This has nothing to do with him*, David thought. *It's between me, Mom and Harry.* He was just about to tell Kelch to mind his own business when his mom said, "Please, Cameron. I want to hear what Mr. Doak has to say."

Harry nodded and continued. "Archie's injuries weren't serious, and in a few days, he was able to rejoin the fighting. After the war was over, we went back to England." Then, with a faraway smile, Harry shared a memory. "I'll never forget V-E Day. May 8th, 1945. The whole country was celebrating, and no place more than London. Parties sprang up everywhere. Bunting was strung from house to house. People danced in the streets. It was an exciting moment, and Archie loved all of it. He didn't want to leave, but I could never stay in England. I couldn't face my past, and Archie understood that more than most. So shortly after V-E Day, we let the army return us to where we'd enlisted, Toronto, and we were demobbed."

"Demobbed?" David's mom said.

"It means being discharged from the army," Kelch explained. "All this is very interesting, I'm sure, but it's ancient history now. Can we get back to the subject at hand, which is this farm?"

Harry's forehead puckered for a moment, then he said, "That's right. Demobbed is short for demobilized. Archie took one look around, declared that Toronto was almost as good as London and decided to stay in the city. I reminded him that he had a farm, family and friends waiting for him, but this time he dug in his heels. He flat-out refused to return to Scotch Gully. Archie had left England for me, so staying in the city was the least I could do."

"But how did you end up here on the farm?" David's mother asked.

Harry closed his eyes and shook his head before continuing. "Archie could see that I hated the city. In the meantime, he was getting letters from his mother, begging him to come home and help on the farm. Two world wars and the polio outbreak had devastated family farms in Scotch Gully; there weren't enough sons left to take over. Archie's parents were desperate for help, but he refused. Archie said that if he went home, even for a visit, he wouldn't have the courage to . . ." Harry's voice trailed off again.

"Courage to what?" David asked. He wondered if that could be what his grandad meant when he'd talked about Mom's graduation? *I wish I had that sort of courage, Davey. It would have been a whole different life for me if I did, but I could never be that brave.* The words sounded right, but something was missing. Grandad's story was about how brave David's mother had been to say no to a marriage she didn't want and to face up to people who didn't approve of her choices. But his grandad would have returned home a war hero, and everyone loves war heroes. It had to be something else.

Harry didn't answer David's question. Instead, Harry said, "Archie loved his parents and didn't want to see them lose the farm, so he wrote them and suggested that I move here and help out in his place."

Kelch said, "You're asking us to believe the Macraths accepted a complete stranger in their home?"

"Not at first. There was some to-ing and fro-ing," Harry admitted. "Archie's father was hurt and angry. He thought his son should come home. But I was used to hard work, and I knew my way around a farm. He soon warmed up to having me around. I think, deep down, both of his parents believed it was a temporary arrangement. I suppose I did too, deep down. Sadly, Archie never returned to Scotch Gully."

"What about his parents? My grandparents? They must have come to the city to see my dad?" David's mother asked.

Harry shook his head. "Archie's mother desperately wanted to. Archie was her only remaining child, but Archie's father wouldn't allow it." Harry shrugged. "That's just the way things were back then. Archie's parents died without ever seeing their son again."

"What about you, Harry?" David asked. "Did you see Grandad again after you moved up here?"

"Yes, David," Harry said. "Every year. The first two weeks in October, we'd meet someplace up north and go fishing."

David's mother whispered, "Dad's fishing trip. That was with you?"

Harry nodded.

In a voice that made it clear to everyone on the porch that he was accusing Harry of something, Kelch said, "Yet after his parents died, you stayed on at the Macrath farm."

"Yes. I stayed," Harry said. "I promised Archie to keep the farm running. For his children," he added.

"Child," Kelch said. "Archibald Macrath had only one child, and he left everything to her. Carla Macrath."

Harry's forehead wrinkled. He turned to David's mom and asked, "What did it say in the will? Did it say your name or . . . ?"

"Of course it did," Kelch interrupted, his voice pitching louder. "It said Carla Macrath in black and white. Not that it's any of your business."

David's mother turned to Kelch with a puzzled look. She placed a hand on his arm. "Cameron, the will said—" but Kelch interrupted her. He put his hand on top of hers as if signalling her to keep quiet. Then he turned back to Harry.

"Look here. Archibald Macrath had only one child. She's sitting right in front of you, and she's telling you to leave by July 1st."

"You can't kick him out, Mom," David pleaded. "What would Grandad say?"

His mother flinched like she'd been slapped. Her skin flushed pink up her neck and across her cheeks.

"Stay out of this," Kelch warned, but David ignored him. He had to make his mother see how wrong it would be to make Harry leave. Grandad had asked Harry to stay, and anyone with eyes could see that Harry had kept his promise to look after the farm. The place was perfect!

David looked at the farmhouse, really looked at it for the first time, with its wide wraparound porch and a main floor that was at least twice as big as his grandfather's house in Cabbagetown. Plus, it had an entire second storey. There had to be at least four bedrooms up there, he figured. Maybe more. Then it hit him — a solution to everyone's problem.

He said, "I get it, Mom. I want to live here too, just as much as you do. Way more, probably. But this is a really big house."

"David?"

"Seriously, Mom. Just look at the place. Why can't we all live here? You, me and Harry. Someone has to run the farm and look after all the animals," David said. "I'm not ready to do that on my own, and you don't know anything about farms. Having Harry stay is the perfect plan!"

"David, what are you talking about? We are not moving to Scotch Gully."

David looked from his mom to Harry to Lizzie, then back to his mom again. "Then why did you bring me all the way here? If we're not moving in, why are you kicking Harry out? What's going on?"

"What's going on, young man," Kelch said, "is that your mother and I are going to develop this land. We're going to build houses. This will be a residential community for people who work in the city."

"No!" David cried. Beside him, Lizzie was near tears.

Harry put out his arms, and Lizzie ran into them, but not before she aimed a fierce look at Kelch.

Harry kissed the top of Lizzie's head. "Archie wanted me here," he said.

"Unfortunately for you, Archibald Macrath is dead, and your say-so won't stand up in court."

"Harry?" Lizzie squeaked.

"It's okay, Lizzie. Don't worry." Harry gave her shoulders a squeeze. He took a deep breath and said, "Mr. Kelch, I have it in writing. Archie put his promise in a letter. It says that I can stay as long as I like."

David whooped. David's mother looked puzzled. Kelch looked like someone who'd just drunk pickle juice straight from the jar.

"I'll need to see that letter," he demanded.

Harry nodded. Gently, he pushed Lizzie away then went inside the farmhouse. For a moment, David thought Lizzie might follow, but then Expo barked, shot off the porch and ran full speed toward the pasture.

"Oh no," Lizzie said. She ran past David to the steps.

"What is it, Lizzie?" David called. "What's happening?"

She stopped, looked over her shoulder. "I think one of the ewes might be in trouble."

"Can I help?"

She hesitated, and David held his breath. After everything that had just happened, would Lizzie trust him? Maybe they couldn't even be friends, now she'd heard what his mom and Kelch were doing to Harry. He chewed his lower lip while he waited for her to answer.

Finally, she said, "Hurry!"

David ran after her.

"David, come back here," his mother yelled.

David ignored her. Kelch barked something also, but by then, David was too far away to hear it. He caught up to Lizzie, and together they ran, with Expo just ahead of them both.

In the pasture, a pregnant ewe bleated so loudly it sounded like she was screaming.

Then her front legs buckled.

"What's going on, Lizzie?" David asked.

"It's Luna. She's a first-time lamber. Usually, the lamb slides out on its own, with the mother's contractions. But some ewes have a hard time, especially if the lamb is big."

Lizzie squatted down, touched her cheek to the ewe's face and made soft whisper-cluck sounds next to her ear. The bleating stopped for a moment, and David worked up the courage to edge closer. With Lizzie at the front calming the animal down, David went to the rear. That's when he saw the lamb.

He knew the general idea of how babies were born. They make everyone take health at school, not to mention that he'd been watching reruns of *Untamed World* since he was a kid, but nothing he'd learned in school or saw on TV prepared him for this. The thing hanging out the ewe's rear end looked nothing like the cute baby lamb he'd expected to see. There was only a large yellow-brown head with a fat tongue dangling out the side of its mouth. Not in a good way either. Not like when a dog hangs his tongue out and pants to cool down.

"Lizzie?"

"Shhh," she said, still crouching by the ewe's head.

"The lamb's head is out."

"Good."

"It's a lot bigger than I thought it would be. There's straw stuck to it. And it kind of smells like poo. Lizzie, do sheep get diarrhea?"

When she heard that, Lizzie stood up and leaned over the ewe's back to look.

"Can you see the legs, David? Under the head?"

"There should be legs?"

"Wait, I'm coming around." In a flash, Lizzie was there crouching beside him. "Oh no!"

"What's wrong, Lizzie?"

"The lamb's stuck. That's why the head's swollen."

"Stuck? What should we do? Pull it out?" David asked, hoping upon hope that her answer would be no.

Lizzie shook her head. "No. We need to push it back inside."

"Are you kidding me?"

She shook her head again. "I need to get Harry to make sure. And I need to get supplies."

"Shouldn't I get Harry?" David didn't like the idea of staying behind with a ewe and lamb that could be dying.

"No. It'll be faster if I go. We need clean rags and some margarine, and I know where all of that stuff is."

"Margarine?" He wasn't sure he'd heard her right.

"David . . . David, are you listening to me?"

He nodded. "Yeah."

"Okay, look. We can't push the lamb back inside the mother if it's covered in straw and poo. She'll get an infection sure as the sun sets. So we're going to have to clean it first. Can you help me do that?"

He wasn't sure. The lamb looked almost dead. He didn't like the idea of touching it.

"David!" Lizzie snapped. "Can you do this or not?"

"Yes," he said. "Yes, I can do it. But I'll need water."

"The pump's over there," she said, pointing. "You'll find a bucket hanging on the handle. Fill it with water, bring it back here fast as you can and start washing it clean."

While Lizzie raced back to the farmhouse, David ran as fast as he could to fetch water.

He'd never used a pump before, but he'd seen one on television and had a fair idea of what to do. He hung the old metal bucket underneath the spout and worked the handle up and down. It moved easily at first, but no water came out. David began to panic. Lizzie had given him one job. Fetch water. He tried pumping faster, but after the fifth or sixth try — he'd lost count — it got stiff. It took everything he had to push the pump handle down. But when he did, the water started flowing.

In no time, the bucket was full. David raced back to the ewe and lamb, trying not to spill the water as he ran. It was impossible. Water sloshed over the top of the bucket, down his shins and onto his only pair of decent sneakers.

When he got back, things looked bleak. David worried he was too late. But he had to try. He wished like crazy that this could have a happy ending, like those TV shows where someone gets pulled from the ocean, then the hero steps in, does CPR, and like magic, they come back to life.

David thought about saying a prayer, but he couldn't remember any. Instead, he offered the only blessing he could think of.

"May the Force be with you."

Then he lifted the bucket and poured water on the lamb's head. Dropping to his knees, he worked his fingers over its head, ears and neck, combing out the biggest ewe berries.

The lamb still didn't move. Desperate, David poured more water over its face. For a few scared seconds, David was convinced he'd been too slow, but as the water rolled over the lamb's face, its eyes fluttered.

The lamb was still alive!

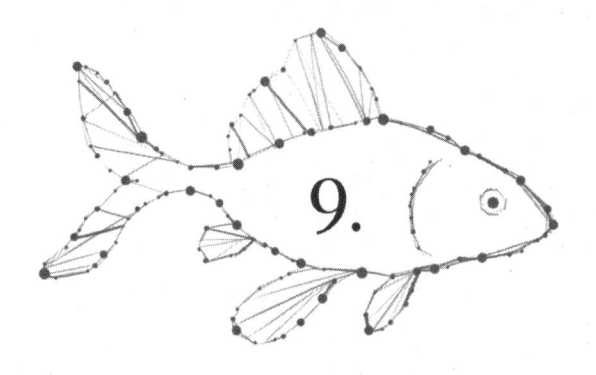

9.

Lizzie

I called for Harry when I got close to the farmhouse. "Harry, come quick!"

Harry hurried to the railing. He was clutching a white envelope.

"What is it? What's wrong, Lizzie?"

Before I could answer, David's mother appeared beside Harry. "Is it David? Is he okay?"

"David's fine," I called back. "Harry, it's one of the ewes. She's giving birth, but her lamb's stuck, and in a bad way."

"How bad?" Harry asked.

"Swollen head, no front legs. Like what happened last year."

I swear Harry sagged when I told him, like the weight of one more piece of bad news was too heavy to carry. Then he said, "Right. We may need to push the lamb back inside to give the ewe a rest."

"That's what I thought. I've got David fetching water and washing the lamb's head. I've come for the clean rags and margarine."

"Good girl. Now go. I'll meet you there." He headed for the porch steps, and I ran for the kitchen.

Inside, I washed my hands, then grabbed a tub of margarine from the fridge and the bag of clean rags that Harry kept on the shelf above the washing machine, before racing back outside.

I caught up to him pretty quickly. Harry runs the way old people do, slow and kind of limpy — more like race walking than running. I slowed right down, but Harry said, "Go, Lizzie. Don't wait for me. Every second counts."

"But what if I'm wrong?"

"Do you think you're wrong?"

I hesitated, then shook my head.

"Then go. I'm right behind you."

"Okay," I said and started running again.

When I got there, David was washing the lamb's face.

"She's still alive, Lizzie."

"Great job, David. Here." I handed him some clean rags. "Use these."

While David wiped the lamb's head, I loaded my hands with gobs of yellow margarine and began the greasing. David helped.

"What's next?" he asked.

"I'll need you to help me push the lamb back inside."

"*Me*? Shouldn't Harry do that?"

"We can't wait for him," I said, running my fingers from the snout to the crown. It felt slick. We were ready.

"Lizzie?" David asked. "Have you ever done this before? Pushed a lamb back inside the mother?"

"Once. Last year. Harry's hands were too big to fit beside the lamb's head."

David was owl-eyed. "*Beside* the head? Like, inside the ewe?"

"I can't do this without you, David!"

He nodded. "It's okay, Lizzie. I'm okay. What do you need me to do?"

"Stand up and grab hold of the fleece on either side of Luna's butt. Really wrap your hands into her fleece. You're going to have to hold her up while I push the lamb. Luna won't like what I'm doing. She may try to lie down."

"Can't we let her lie down if she wants to? I mean, if it makes her more comfortable . . . ?"

"I need her standing, David. If she's standing, there's more space for me to push the lamb back inside."

David nodded and I stroked the lamb's head while I waited for him to get in position.

"Ready!" David said.

"Here I go." Flattening the lamb's ears back to make it more streamlined, I slid my hands alongside the lamb's head and inside Luna. The ewe wasn't pushing back. That was good for me. But she was trying to lie down and that wasn't good.

"Keep her standing, David!"

I held my breath, said a prayer for strength, and pushed that lamb all the way back inside its mom.

That's when I noticed Harry. He'd climbed over the fence and was panting like a dog after a big run. He leaned forward, hands on his knees, gulping in drinks of air. I stopped worrying about Luna and her lamb and started worrying about Harry.

David must have been thinking the same thing because he whispered, "Is Harry okay?"

"I dunno," I whispered back.

Harry lifted his head. "I'm fine, kids." There was nothing wrong with his hearing.

I'd never thought much about it before, but Harry was getting old. I was glad he had that letter from David's grandfather saying he could stay here. I didn't want to think about what would happen to him if he had to leave.

Harry knelt down beside me. He found a pair of rubber gloves in the rag bag and pulled them on.

"Great work, kids. I'm going to reach in now and find the lamb's front legs. Then I'll pull the lamb. Keep holding on, David. You're doing a great job. Just keep her standing, son."

Harry got to work. A few minutes later, we had a lamb, and it was my turn. I started to rub the lamb dry.

"David," Harry said, "see if Luna will lick your hands."

"She's doing it!"

"That's a good sign. Lizzie?"

I knew what Harry wanted. I moved the lamb next to Luna's nose. Most times a ewe will start licking her lamb's head all on her own. It clears the mucous. Luna was licking David hand's all right, but she didn't make a move toward her lamb.

"The lamb's just lying there, Lizzie," David whispered. "What should we do?"

I placed my hand on David's arm, careful not to startle Luna while she was licking his hand, then pushed his arm down, moving it closer to the lamb. David caught on right away.

"Go slow," I whispered.

David coaxed Luna's head all the way down to her lamb then slowly moved his hand away and Luna took a first few licks of her baby, just like a ewe should.

"David, you're a star!"

"So she's going to be okay?" David asked looking worried and hopeful at the same time.

"He," I said. "It's a ram lamb."

I looked to Harry. "What do you think, Harry?"

"I'll get Doc Cousins to come and check mother and son, but this was a fine day's work. I'm very grateful to you both."

Then Harry looked from David to me, then back to David again. "David, what you and Lizzie did . . . your grandfather would have been so proud."

We all stood up and took a few steps back to give the new family some room. I turned to give David a smile and a shoulder check, but when I saw him, really saw him, I burst out laughing. David was a mud-ball, brown from his belly to his sneakers, and he was grinning ear to ear like he'd won the top prize at the 4-H. I threw my arms around him as if we were the oldest of friends and not two kids who'd only just met.

It didn't feel weird at all; it felt right. When I let go, we were both grinning like Cheshire cats.

"Now I *know* you're a goldfish, David. How many city kids could have done what you just did?"

"Thanks, Lizzie." David turned to Harry, and his smile faded. "What about you, Harry? What's going to happen to you?"

"Don't you worry about me, David. Your grandfather took good care of me. I've got his letter, remember?"

"Good," David said. "Because if Grandad wanted you to live here, Harry, so do I."

Harry's eyes were shiny from the tears that were forming. "Thank you, David. That means the world to me."

A voice bellowed in the distance. "Let's go!"

I looked up. David's mother had followed us to the pasture and was standing just outside the fence, wide-eyed and watching everything. It was Kelch who'd yelled. He was back by the farmhouse, but heading our way at a clip. When he arrived at the fence, he announced, "We're leaving. Let's go, Carla."

"Not yet, Mom. Please?" David pleaded. "I want to stay and see if the lamb is okay."

She hesitated and looked at Kelch. "Maybe we could stay?"

Kelch slipped his arm around her waist and kissed the top of her head. She nodded then turned to David. "Come on, David. Time to go."

David didn't argue with her, but he might as well have. He crossed his arms across his chest, pressed his lips together and stuck his chin way out in what my grandma would call a try-and-make-me pose. Then, before I could blink, Kelch was over the fence and inside the pasture. With his stilt-long legs, crossing the barbed wire must have been as easy for him as stepping over a curb.

"When I tell you to do something, you do it," Kelch said, and grabbed David's arm.

"Or what?" David demanded. Kelch must have squeezed his arm hard then, because David yipped. "Ow!"

Kelch leaned way down so that his long horse-face was so close to David that their noses almost touched. David's mom was still on the other side of the fence, but I was just close enough to hear Kelch spit-whisper, "I'll be damned if I let you ruin this for me. Mark my words, I am going to send you to a boarding school so far from the city that you won't even be able to come home on weekends. How's that for an 'or what?'" Then Kelch stood up and, still holding David's arm, announced in a voice loud enough for David's mother to hear, "Do we understand each other, young man?"

I wanted nothing more at that moment than to wind up and kick Kelch right in the shins, but like a coward, I just stood there and did nothing while Kelch dragged David to the fence, only letting go long enough for both to cross.

David looked over his shoulder at me and Harry with a face so miserable it hurt to see. I desperately wanted to do something to cheer him up. Then I remembered the eggs.

"Wait," I yelled. "Don't go yet."

I slipped between the fence wires and raced to the kitchen. I grabbed the DAVID carton of eggs with my phone number inside.

By the time I got back outside, David, his mother and Kelch were already at the car. The trunk was wide open. David's mother was tearing holes in a green garbage bag while David took off his mucky sneakers and slipped on some rubber boots.

"Put this on, David," she said.

Kelch barked at David to hurry and get in the car. When he saw me, Kelch plucked the egg carton right out of my hands.

"Those are for David!" I protested.

"Fine," Kelch said and passed the eggs to David, who was already seated in the back wearing his garbage bag. "I don't want to see one speck of dirt on my upholstery. Understood?" Kelch told him, then climbed into the driver's seat, started the car and backed up.

David looked like a beat dog. But he wasn't. David was a goldfish. I knew that in my heart.

I made my hand into a phone — thumb at my ear, pinky at my chin — and I mouthed, "Call me," just as Kelch turned, stepped on the gas and sped away down the drive.

* * *

Harry was in the kitchen talking to Doc Cousins on the telephone when I heard my grandma's car come up the drive. I stuck my head out the screen door to let her know where we were.

She came inside, shaking her head and saying,

"Some big fancy car just peeled out of here like the very devil himself was chasing its tail."

I stifled a laugh because my grandma was famous for having a lead foot of her own. Mom and I have a secret pact never to talk to Grandma about anything important when she's behind the wheel. When Grandma gets angry or excited about something, she steps on the gas pedal hard. That's not the worst of it. Grandma can get so caught up in a conversation that she forgets she's driving, and she'll turn to look at you. When she does that, the car heads where she looks. Mom and I made our pact because we didn't want to end up in a ditch.

"Hello, Emma," Harry said.

"Hello, Harry," she answered. Me, she grabbed by the shoulders and held still so she could plant a fat kiss on my forehead.

"Who was that leaving here? Some salesman you chased off with old Mrs. Macrath's shotgun?" Grandma said with a chortle.

I didn't find that funny. Not anymore. Not since I'd met an actual Macrath and learned that Archie Macrath was not just some boy in an old photo. He was David's grandfather and — this was the biggest, most important, most unforgettable thing of all — this farm belonged to the Macraths. Not Harry. I had so many questions for my grandma that I didn't know where to start. I turned to Harry expecting him to fill her in on everything that had happened since I got off the school bus, but all Harry said was, "Are we still on for Sunday night, Emma?"

"Dinner and the Royal Canadian Air Farce on the CBC? Of course," she answered. "Wouldn't miss it."

What the heck? Why was Harry making plans and small talk instead of telling Grandma about how Kelch was trying to kick him off the farm?

Grandma turned to me and said, "Looks like it's just you and me for a bit, Lizzie. Your mom has to stay in the city."

Before I could open my mouth, Harry snuck in with a question. "Did Susan say how it's going?"

"Harry?" I said, nudging him to tell Grandma about what had just happened.

He just shot me a funny look, like he wanted me to keep quiet. That didn't make any sense at all.

"But, Harry?" I said.

"Not now, Lizzie. Go on, Emma. Tell us about Susan."

"She's certainly charged up and ready for the fight. She's got a meeting tomorrow with Alan Borovoy at the CCLA."

Curiosity got the better of me. "What's the CCLA?"

"It's where your mother used to work, Lizzie.

The Canadian Civil Liberties Association. Now shake a leg, young lady."

I begged, "You have to tell her, Harry."

"Tell me what?" Grandma asked.

Harry just stood there. I rolled my eyes. "Grandma, did you know that the farm doesn't belong to Harry?"

Grandma's eyes went goggle-wide. "Elizabeth Colleen Ross, wherever did you hear that?"

"From a horrible man named Kelch. That was his car that squealed out of here. But, Grandma, Harry said it was true. He said the farm belonged to his friend Archie Macrath. Or, well, it used to."

"Used to?" Grandma swallowed hard, once, twice. Harry nodded. Grandma pulled out a chair and sat down. Her face was the colour of milk.

"Grandma? Are you okay?"

Harry pulled up a chair next to her and sat down. He placed a hand on top of hers. She grabbed it and held on tight.

"He's gone, Emma."

"Archie's gone," she repeated in a voice that was barely more than a whisper. "And you didn't know, Harry?"

Harry shook his head. "Not until today."

"But the farm . . . ?"

Harry shook his head. "Apparently, there's a new will that names Carla. She inherits everything."

"Oh, Harry!" Now Grandma put her other hand on top of Harry's like some hand sandwich.

Hand sandwich. Ham sandwich. Any other time that would have made me giggle. Not now.

"You knew him, didn't you, Grandma? You knew Archie Macrath."

I didn't tell her about the photograph I'd found tucked into the library book. I didn't know why, but something told me to keep that piece of information to myself for now.

Grandma cleared her throat and sat up a little straighter. One moment I could see right through to the hurt inside of her. The next it was like she'd slipped on a mask. She was back to the strong, always-do-the-right-thing grandma I was used to.

"Did I know Archie Macrath?" she asked. "Well, of course I did, Lizzie. Everyone knows everyone in Scotch Gully, don't they?" She let out a small snort. "You think this town is small now, you should have seen it when I was a girl."

"So you and Archie Macrath were friends?" I knew they were from the photograph. More than friends, I guessed.

"Oh, yes," Grandma said. "I can even tell you the exact moment our friendship began. I was five years old and terrified to start school."

"Scared of school? Really?" This was a story I'd never heard before. "How come?"

"Because, Lizzie, there had been a polio outbreak there."

Grandma must have seen the alarm on my face because she said, "Don't worry. That was a lifetime ago, long before they had the vaccine. And even back then, once we understood how the disease spread, the outhouses were removed and indoor washrooms with running water for handwashing were installed. There hasn't been a case since."

"Your sister had polio, didn't she?"

"Yes. She was partially paralyzed and used two forearm crutches to walk. Archie Macrath's two older brothers got it too. They both died, and that fact was never far from my mind. I was terrified that when I went to school, I would get sick."

"Then why did you go?"

"It was the law, young lady. Yes, even back then. By the time I arrived at the schoolhouse on my first day, I was sobbing, begging my mother to take me home. When Eileen Budge saw me carrying on like that, she pointed at me, laughed and called me names. They were ridiculous names and shouldn't have mattered, but to a five-year-old, they were hurtful."

"Bethany Budge's grandma," I muttered.

Grandma nodded.

"I swear, those Budges are born mean," I said.

"Mean isn't something you're born with, Lizzie.

It's not like having red hair or green eyes. Mean is something you learn."

I wasn't so sure about that, but I didn't want a lecture. I wanted to hear the story about Grandma and Archie Macrath. "So what happened next?"

"Well, as I said, Eileen Budge made fun of me, and the other children laughed. All except Archie. He walked right up to me on the playground, took my hand and held it tight all day."

I saw Harry give my grandma's hand a squeeze. I wondered, not for the first time, why Harry and my grandma never got married. They were both alone, and they were friends. Best friends. They spent most of their free time together. But all I said was, "That's really sweet."

"He had his flaws, Archie Macrath did, but he was the gentlest boy I've ever met," Grandma said.

Harry nodded.

"And you stayed friends all through school?"

"Oh, yes. From first grade right through twelfth. Those last few years, Archie Macrath was my boyfriend."

I had already guessed that from the photograph, but I still didn't tell her about it. I wanted to hear what she had to say.

"When was the last time you saw him, Grandma?"

"June 29th, 1940."

"Whoa! You remember the actual date?"

"I do because it was the night of our high school graduation. Back then, high school graduations were second in importance only to weddings and births."

"Really?"

Graduating wasn't a big deal now, in 1981. Even in Scotch Gully, where lots of kids still stayed on to work their family farms, finishing high school wasn't special. Parents expected their kids to graduate these days. Grade twelve at least. Maybe it was different in Grandma's day.

Grandma's eyes went all dreamy. "Archie was my escort to the graduation dance," she said. "All the girls wore white dresses. Most of our classmates married right after high school, and those dresses we all wore to graduation, with a tweak here and a tweak there, became our wedding dresses."

"Grandma, you didn't expect to marry Archie Macrath, did you?"

Grandma looked over at Harry, and they smiled at one another, kind of sad. Old people do that a lot when they remember stuff.

"Yes," she said. "But it wasn't just me being a silly teenage girl. I'd wager that the whole town expected Archie and I would graduate, get married, and then Archie would take over his family farm. There was no one but Archie."

"Because he'd lost both his older brothers to polio?"

"That's right, Lizzie." Grandma seemed far away again. She shook her head and said, "You know, I loved that dress. I sewed it myself on my grandmother's old Singer 28 sewing machine. Goodness, but that thing was an antique even in 1940, with its cast-iron legs and treadle. It didn't need electricity, you know."

Sewing and sewing machines didn't interest me at all. Learning everything I could about Archie Macrath, *that* was interesting.

"What happened, Grandma? Why did you two break up? Did you have a fight?"

"With Archie? Goodness no. Archie never fought with anyone. He was far too sweet. And he hated confrontation of any kind. If he saw a fight coming, that boy would turn one hundred and eighty degrees and head the other way."

I could sympathize with that. I hated confrontation too. "Then what happened?" I asked.

"Well, the morning after our graduation dance, Archie up and hitchhiked to Toronto and enlisted in the army without telling a soul. It was a shocker, I can tell you, and not just for me. For everyone in town. Archie Macrath was the very last person you'd ever expect would sign up to fight in a war. He couldn't use a gun on an animal, couldn't even kill a hen when it had stopped laying and was destined for the stew-pot. No one could picture him turning a gun on a person. But fight in the war he did."

That clinched it. It *was* David's grandfather who bought Harry that meal and a room at the YMCA. This was getting weirder and weirder by the minute, and I had an itch about it all that I had to scratch.

"Were you sad when he left, Grandma?"

"Heartbroken," she said. "But I reminded myself that Archie was being brave. He was serving King and country. I had to do my part also — be brave and wait for him to return."

"I remember this part of the story," I said. "Right after graduation, you went to Vancouver to live with your sister, Irene." I'd heard this a ton of times. Because of her polio, Grandma's big sister, Irene, had moved to Vancouver — a city with buses and taxis and no icy winter sidewalks, where she could be independent.

But Grandma shook her head. "Not until September. Archie's parents were devastated when he enlisted. They were worried about him, and they were left shorthanded on the farm, so I stayed the summer to help them. After all those years, and growing up just a mile from this place, the Macraths were like family."

I had a crazy idea playing hide-and-seek in my

brain, but this notion of mine was like a skittish animal — every time I reached for it, it slinked away. I needed to let the idea come to me on its own, so I smiled my best smile, shrugged my shoulders and said, "You know, Grandma, I'd really love to see that graduation dress you sewed yourself. Do you still have it?"

"Goodness no. I have no idea where that old thing is."

"You must have some pictures of you wearing it, Grandma. Like maybe at your graduation? With Archie Macrath?"

Grandma clicked her tongue against her teeth. "Elizabeth Colleen Ross, what's really going on?"

I shrugged. "I guess it's all this family tree stuff that has me curious."

That was true, but there was more to it than that. What Grandma just said about moving to Vancouver didn't line up with the story I knew — the one I'd heard my whole life. In the old version, the one Grandma had been telling forever, she left for Vancouver at the end of June, right after she graduated high school. She was supposed to get off the train in Vancouver on Dominion Day, bump into Phillip Ross and fall in love at first sight, get engaged ten days later, and marry him the day after that. Then, after Phillip Ross got shipped off to Italy, she was supposed to discover she was pregnant.

But Grandma had just said she'd stayed in Scotch Gully for the whole summer and didn't go to Vancouver until September, and that didn't make sense.

My mom was born on April 1st — eight pounds, eight ounces. I'd watched her write that in the family Bible only yesterday. But if Grandma didn't meet Phillip Ross until September, shouldn't my mom have been born in early June and not April 1st like she was?

"Grandma," I said, "Archie Macrath's grandson was at Harry's today. His name is David. I really like him."

"Lizzie!" Grandma's eye's bugged wide.

"Relax, Grandma. I don't like him like that. David and I, we're kind of . . . well . . . we're friends now." Then I thought of something I could say that she'd believe, Harry too, and would buy me some time to wrangle this crazy idea of mine. "David misses his grandad. I think he'd love to see pictures. Harry said David is the spitting image of his grandfather. Isn't that right, Harry?"

"He is indeed."

"He's got bright orange hair and freckles. Like Mom."

"Is that so?" Grandma said, standing up. "My goodness, it's getting late. We need to get home. I have to get dinner started, and you need to get a start on that social studies project. I stopped at the

Mercantile and got your Bristol board."

I groaned.

"Let's go, young lady," she said. "Your project isn't going to finish itself." Grandma patted me on the head then walked past me toward the farmhouse door. Then she turned to Harry and asked, "Are you going to be okay?"

"Archie took care of me," Harry said. "I have his letter."

I flashed back to earlier, to when I'd run back for the margarine and clean rags. I remembered Harry coming to the railing holding something in his hands. The letter.

"Where is it, Harry?"

"The letter? It's on the porch."

I ran through the house and out the front door. I couldn't see the letter anywhere on the porch. I checked the yard in case a gust of wind had caught it and blown it over the railing. Nothing. And with the grass so green and the sun so bright, a white envelope would have stood out.

Harry looked puzzled. He patted his pockets. No letter. His forehead creased.

"I thought I left it on the chair. It must be here somewhere," he said. "Check under the cushions."

We all looked, but there was no trace of Harry's letter anywhere.

"I must have dropped it when I was running to

the ewe," he said. "I'll go look."

"We'll help you," said Grandma.

"No. You take Lizzie home, Emma. It's a school night, and she's got things to do."

"Six eyes are better than two," Grandma said.

Even if we had sixty eyes, I was pretty sure we wouldn't find Harry's letter. While we were saving the ewe, Kelch had stayed behind. I'd bet the farm that he took it. I bet Kelch stole Harry's letter.

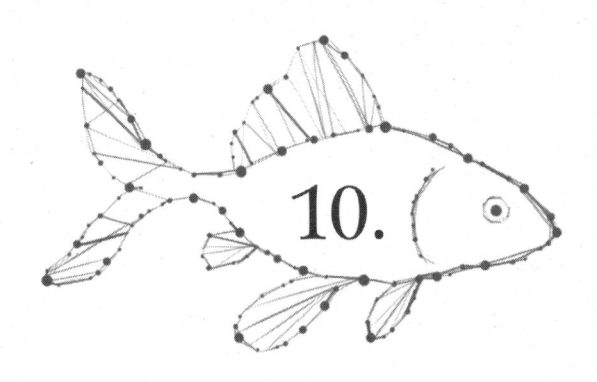

10.

David

David watched Lizzie from the backseat of Kelch's car. Of all the lousy, horrible, rotten things that had happened to him recently, and there had been a lot of rotten stuff, Lizzie was something good. David marvelled that she would want to stay friends after Kelch had tried to evict Harry, especially after hearing Kelch's plan to level the farm. But there she stood with her hand beside her ear, thumb and pinky finger sticking out like she was holding a telephone, signalling him to call her. As Kelch peeled out of the driveway, David looked down at the egg carton with his name written across the top, and he opened the lid.

Inside, in the middle of the carton, was the egg with Lizzie's phone number. Right below her number was the outline of a fish — kind of like the ones you see all the time in the city on bumper stickers.

His grandfather used to call them Bible fish. But instead of printing JESUS inside this fish, Lizzie had made a capital D. For David.

Because Lizzie thinks I'm a goldfish.

David felt a smile fill his lungs and work its way to his face.

Until Kelch barked.

"Do you have any idea what you could have cost us back there?"

David closed the egg carton and chewed his lower lip.

"Well, do you?" Kelch demanded. David saw Kelch's eyes dart to the rearview mirror.

When David didn't answer, Kelch said, "We have plans for that land."

"We? *We*?" David said, his voice pitching higher. Kelch's threat about boarding school was still fresh, but this was just too much for David. "*We* is Mom and me," he cried. "You aren't part of us. When are you going to get that through your fat head?"

Some people flush pink when they get mad. Some go a splotchy red. Kelch turned purple from the neck up, and with his long face and fat forehead, he looked like an upside-down eggplant. David knew he'd crossed a line. He looked to his mother, not because he expected her to defend him — lately, she'd been a loyal stormtrooper to Kelch's Grand Moff Tarkin — but David needed to know how angry she was. It was like she hadn't heard a word he'd said. She just sat there still as a statue with her cheek pressed against the side window. David had the same habit. He liked the way the glass felt cool against his face.

Then, out of the blue and almost like she was telling a bedtime story, his mother said, "Once upon a time in Ripon, in the north of England, there was a little boy. When he was just a baby, the boy's mother sold him to some street performers, who put him to work. The boy's job was to shake a tin cup at the people who passed by."

Kelch whipped his head around to look at her.

"What the heck, Carla?"

"It's a story my father used to tell me when I was a little girl."

"And you're telling me now because . . . ?"

"Because I think the boy in my father's story was Harry."

"That's ridiculous," Kelch said.

Kelch squeezed the steering wheel like he wanted to crush it into dust. His shoulders went stiff, a vein in his neck bulged blue and his head became an eggplant again. David shrank back in his seat as far as he could. This was the Kelch his mother never saw; the Kelch who frightened David. But his mother wasn't looking, and Kelch quickly relaxed his grip on the wheel.

"It sounds like a story your father told you to make you behave," Kelch said. "A classic cautionary tale. Like 'Little Red Riding Hood' warning children not to talk to strangers. 'Be a good girl, or I'll sell you to the street performers just like that little boy from Ripon.'"

"That doesn't sound like my father," she said, shaking her head. "In his story, the boy was a hero. He sailed to a faraway land, like Harry. He was unjustly imprisoned and had to escape like Harry did from that farm. He fought evil, and he rescued a prince."

"Like Harry fighting the Nazis and saving Grandad on Juno Beach!" David said. "It is about Harry, Mom. Lizzie told me all about it."

His mother twisted around to look at him. "Really? What did she say?"

The story Harry told his mother on the porch had begun when he'd run away from the farm in Saskatchewan. David told her everything he could remember about Harry's life before that.

"Oh, please!" Kelch said. "A mother selling her child for a bottle of liquor? British home children? Child slaves? Carla, that story is a complete fantasy from start to finish."

"I didn't say Harry was a slave," David protested. "Lizzie called it something else. Something about . . . I can't remember. It sounded like false teeth."

He wished he could remember the word because from the front seat, Kelch let out a derisive snort.

"If that old man told you he was the love child of Mata Hari and King George V, you'd probably believe him," Kelch said. "You swallow every fish tale you're told, hook, line and sinker. Life isn't one of your TV shows or comic books." Then Kelch turned to David's mother. "Carla, I have never heard of British home children. Not once in high school or during my six years of university. I read the papers every day, and I've never seen that mentioned once. Have you?"

"No. But . . . but what if it's true?" she asked.

Kelch snorted again, but when he saw the look on David's mother's face, he softened. "It's not true, Carla. But even if it was, it shouldn't make a difference to us."

"But it does, Cam," she said.

"For God's sake, why?"

"Because of that farm. It's not an overgrown piece of land with a tumbledown farmhouse. It's charming, and it's someone's home. It's Harry Doak's home, the man who saved my father's life." David's mother shook her head. "It doesn't matter now anyway. The development idea is over. Mr. Doak says he has a letter from my father giving him permission to stay."

"Don't you worry your pretty head about that,"

Kelch said, patting her knee. He looked suspiciously smug. "The letter won't be a problem."

"How do you know that?"

"I just do. I don't want you to worry about anything, sweetheart. I'll take care of it all. That's all you need to know." Kelch smiled and took a deep breath. "That land is our future. You just have to look around you at what's happening out there to see that. Toronto has become too expensive for regular Joes. These days, people are willing to commute long distances just to be able to raise their families in a nice house in a nice neighbourhood. That piece of farmland is a good commuter distance for a subdivision, and it's the perfect size for our first project. It's even better than I could have hoped for. This is a win-win, sweetheart. We develop that land, and not only will we be giving hundreds of families their dream, but we'll also be set for life."

"Maybe you're right, Cameron. Still, before I do anything, I need to think about it some more."

David gripped the egg carton in his hands and pressed his lips together to stop himself from giving a cheer. His mother said *I*, not *we*.

* * * *

Soon they were back in the city. Kelch pulled into the small lot behind Rosehill Realty. The second he turned off the engine, David had the car door open.

"Careful getting out," Kelch snapped. "Not one

speck of dirt on those seats, do you hear me?"

"Yes, sir." David slid slowly out of the back seat, scooching the plastic garbage bag beneath him as he inched across. When he'd stood up, Kelch asked, "Do you have your house keys?"

"Yeah?"

"Good." The trunk popped open. Kelch said, "Get your dirty shoes, then go inside and clean up. I have something important to talk to your mother about. And remember, don't slam the trunk. Let the motor do it."

"Yeah, yeah," David muttered under his breath.

His shoes were a gooey mess. He peeled off the garbage bag he'd been wearing and used it to pick them up. Wrapping the shoes inside the dark green plastic, he closed the trunk just far enough that the pull-down motor engaged, closing the trunk the rest of the way. When he looked up, he was surprised to see his mother standing by the back of the car.

"I'll take those," she said, reaching for his sneakers. "I better wash these tonight, don't you think?"

"I'm sorry, Mom," David said. "I didn't have time to go back and put on my rubber boots. The ewe was in trouble and—"

"It's okay, David," she said. "I saw what you did. I'm very proud of you. And, David, after everything that's happened today, I think you and I need to sit down and talk about your grandfather. He and I didn't always agree or approve of each other's choices, but I loved him. You know that, right?"

He nodded.

"Good. What do you say we start right now?"

"Now? I thought you had to talk about something important with . . ."

"Cam and I can talk later. Your grandfather was important too. And so are you."

David grinned so wide his face hurt.

A car door slammed. "I'm going to my office," Kelch announced, his face a dark cloud.

"All right," his mother said. Her forehead wrinkled like she was upset, but then she smiled at David and tipped her head toward the door. "Shall we?"

An hour later, David was showered, his mucky clothes and shoes were in the washing machine, and he was sitting beside his mother on the sofa surrounded by old photographs of his grandparents.

"That's Grandma Maeve, right?" David asked. "She was really pretty. You look a lot like her."

"And you look just like your grandfather." His mother smiled and ruffled his hair.

"You don't ever talk about your mom," David said. "How come?"

"Honestly, she was complicated and it can be painful to think about her. I do remember that she was difficult, really volatile. She'd be happy one minute — higher than a kite and doing three things at once — and the next, she'd take to her bed crying and not come out for days. Your grandfather was patient as a saint with her."

"That sounds like Grandad," David said.

His mother nodded.

"What was wrong with her, Mom?"

"Back then, they called it female hysteria. I don't know what it really was."

Just then a wonderful smell wafted up the staircase. He'd had a snack after his shower, but that aroma of salty melted cheese made David's stomach rumble. Seconds later, Kelch walked into the apartment carrying a pizza box.

"You brought dinner?" his mother said.

"For David. They just delivered it." Kelch headed into the kitchen with the pizza. David could hardly believe it.

Kelch put the box on the kitchen table, adding a plate and cutlery from the drying rack. Then he turned to David's mother.

"For you and me, sweetheart, there is a reservation at Ed's Warehouse tonight. So go fix your makeup, put on your prettiest dress and your highest heels. This is a special occasion."

"Special?" she asked.

"I have something very important to talk to you about," Kelch said, patting his pocket. David noticed a lump. For a split-second, he worried that

Kelch had found his sock-full-of-coins — his runaway money — but one look at his mother's face and David knew it must be something else. Her eyes were opened wide, and her mouth made a small "o" shape. She looked like a kid who'd been promised a puppy.

"Will you be okay, David?" she asked. When he didn't answer right away, she said, "Pizza for dinner is pretty special too. You love pizza, right?"

He could tell she really wanted to go. David nodded. She rewarded him with a kiss on the forehead before disappearing down the hall with Kelch following close behind. When they returned, they were both spit and polished and wearing fancy clothes like they were going to a wedding. Kelch carried a camera.

Before David could ask, Kelch thrust the camera into his hands, saying, "Take a picture of us. I want to record this special day."

Then they were gone, his mother's high heels click-clacking down the stairs. David waited until he heard the car start and the tires crunch over the parking lot gravel. Then he carried the pizza box into the living room and turned on the television. He didn't care that he was grounded from watching TV or that Kelch had threatened to send him away to boarding school if he did one more thing wrong. Kelch wasn't here.

He ate his pizza in front of a *Star Trek* rerun. It was cold now, but he didn't care. When he was full, he carried the rest of the box into the kitchen and put it into the fridge. That's when he spotted Lizzie's eggs. He'd put them in the refrigerator before he'd had his shower.

David picked up the carton and carried it to the wall phone in the kitchen. Careful to get all the numbers right, he dialed Lizzie. She picked up on the second ring.

"It's okay, Grandma. I've got it," he heard Lizzie call before she'd even said hello.

Lizzie's grandmother must have been close by because David heard her too, clear as a bell. "If it's for me, Lizzie, take a message. I'm going to lie down for a bit."

"Sure, Grandma," she said.

"Lizzie, it's me. David."

"I figured it was," she said. She must have her hand cupped around the mouthpiece because the next words that came out sounded like she was inside a cave. "Boy, oh boy, am I'm glad you called."

"I wasn't sure you'd ever talk to me again after hearing what my mom and Kelch are trying to do to Harry."

"That's them. Not you. You stuck up for Harry. David, would you really want to live there at the farm with him?"

David nodded, then he realized Lizzie couldn't see him. "I meant it," he said.

"Good," Lizzie said. "Because I need your help."

"Help with what?" David asked.

"Harry's letter. It's gone. He thinks he dropped somewhere but—"

"You think Kelch took it, don't you?" David said.

"I do."

David chewed his bottom lip. What Lizzie said made sense. Kelch was a snake. Stealing that letter, the one that his grandad wrote to Harry saying he could live at the farm, was a low-down thing to do, and there was nothing lower than a snake's belly.

"David?" Lizzie interrupted his thinking. "Are you there?"

"Yeah. I'm here."

"I'm sure I'm right. Kelch didn't come to the pasture, remember? He only showed up at the very end, and then he was in a big hurry to leave."

David hadn't noticed it at the time, but Lizzie was right. Then there was the ride home. When his mother mentioned the letter, Kelch had said, "I'll take care of it. That's all you need to know."

Maybe "take care of it" meant that Kelch had taken the letter.

"David, are you there?"

"Yeah, I am. And, Lizzie," David said, "I think you're right. In fact, I'm sure of it."

"Harry needs that letter, David. Can you help us?"

David looked down at the egg in his hand, saw Lizzie's drawing of a goldfish and decided.

"I think so," he said. "Kelch won't want my mom to know he took the letter. He will have hidden it somewhere. In his office, probably."

"Oh no!" Her disappointment was evident, even over the phone.

"No, that's good. Our apartment is above the office," David explained. "They're out to dinner now, so I can go downstairs and look for it."

"Really? That's awesome! Call me when you find it. We need to get it to my mom. She's a lawyer. She'll know what to do. And, David?"

"Yeah?"

"Thanks. I'm glad you're my friend."

* * * *

Harry's letter was surprisingly easy to find. Still inside its original envelope, the letter lay on top of a small pile of papers that included the last will and testament of David's grandfather and a very official-looking eviction notice for Harry. That's what Kelch really came to his office to do, David realized. Not to be a nice guy and order him pizza; he came here to write the eviction notice. It made David angry, but not as angry as seeing his grandfather's will on Kelch's desk. That made David's blood boil. The will was family stuff, and Kelch. Was. Not. Family.

David reached for it, but he moved too quickly and knocked over the only knick-knack in Kelch's entire office — a china basket with pink porcelain roses that looked like something an old lady would have, not something that look-at-me-I'm-such-a-big-man Kelch would keep on his desk. The basket hit at an awkward angle, breaking off a china rose. The old David would have flinched, worried what Kelch would do when he spotted it. But this David was a goldfish.

Still, when he righted the china basket, David spun it partway around, hoping Kelch wouldn't spot the damage. That's when he saw what had been sitting underneath. It was the fat stack of boarding school brochures. At the very top of the stack was an application, filled in by Kelch and ready to mail. He must have done that when he was waiting for the pizza. Even though it wasn't cold inside Kelch's office, David felt a shiver run down his back and gooseflesh rise on his arms.

He wanted to rip that application up and throw it in the trash, just like he wanted to tear up Harry's eviction notice, but he couldn't do either, because Kelch would notice and figure out who'd done it. Then, David's mouth twitched up at the corners. He had an idea that might slow Kelch down.

David took the eviction notice and slipped it underneath the boarding school brochures.

"Kelch will go nuts trying to find this. He'll think he accidentally put it there himself."

Now there was only the envelope with Harry's letter and the will. David picked up the letter. It made him feel strange to see his grandfather's handwriting again. He knew that if he read the letter, he would hear his grandfather's voice in his head, but opening it seemed like snooping. Like looking in his mother's purse — something he was never supposed to do. So David placed the envelope to the side and picked up the will. It was thin, only a few pages.

THE LAST WILL & TESTAMENT

of

ARCHIBALD CONALL MACRATH

NOVEMBER 24, 1948

David placed a finger across his grandfather's name and held it there for a long moment before he started to read.

I, Archibald Conall Macrath, bequeath all my worldly possessions to be divided equally among my present and future children.

"Kelch, you are such a liar!" David said aloud. "You told Harry that the will named my mom, but it doesn't. It just says children."

What it actually said was "present and future children" and that, David thought, was strange. It made it sound like his grandfather already had kids when he made his will, but David knew that wasn't true. His mother wasn't born until 1950, two years after this will. It was puzzling, but he guessed this was just the way lawyers talked. Lizzie's mom would know. She's a lawyer. He could ask her.

David put the will down and picked up the envelope with Harry's letter once more. His grandfather's handwriting was unmistakable. David knew it almost as well as his own.

He wanted to take the letter, envelope and all, and send it back to Harry. He could do that. He'd have to hide it somewhere in his room until he wasn't grounded anymore, until he could put the whole thing inside a new envelope with Harry's address, use the coins from his sock to buy stamps at 7-Eleven, and stick the whole thing into a mailbox. In less than a week, Harry's letter would be on its way back to its rightful owner.

Except for one super-sized problem. Kelch. If David took the letter, there would be two things missing — the letter and the eviction notice. Kelch would notice that for sure. While David considered what to do, he turned the envelope over and over.

"What if I take out only one page?" he thought out loud. "If I just take the page where Grandad tells Harry he can stay, then put the rest of the letter back inside the envelope, I bet Kelch wouldn't notice for ages."

The idea seemed so simple and so right to David. Harry would be safe, Lizzie would be happy, and David would be helping honour his grandfather's promise to Harry. David took a deep breath and slipped out the fat fold of papers.

There was a date at the top of the letter. November 24th, 1948. That was curious. His grandfather wrote this letter the same day he'd made his will. David began to read.

My Dearest Love,

Wait. This can't be Harry's letter, David thought. It was his grandfather's handwriting, no mistake, but this was a love letter. Confused but curious, David read on.

This is a difficult letter to write, but first I have to thank you for the photographs of Susan. They mean the world to me. Seven years old. She's growing up so fast, and with every letter you send, I'm reminded of what a mess I've made of everything. I know I should come home, but I can't, Harry. Even though my parents are gone now, I just can't. Each time I imagine returning to Scotch Gully, I feel a choking sensation like I'm drowning under the weight of other people's expectations. I never asked to take over the farm. I never wanted to be a farmer. I never wanted that life. It's what I ran away from.

David blinked once, then twice. This was a letter to Harry, but . . .

It's mostly what I ran away from. I just can't face Emma or the child. If I return, it's not only the farm I'll have to take on, it's her. She will expect to marry. Can you see how that makes everything even harder? I do love Emma, in my own way, and I would dearly love to know my daughter, but if I come back now, it would mean locking myself in that cage for the rest of my life. And worse, you would be agonizingly close, but out of reach. I'm not brave enough for that. I just can't face it, Harry. You must think I'm a coward, and I suppose I am, especially compared to what you've had to endure in your life. But that is who I am. That's the real face of the person you fell in love with.

His grandfather's words, the words David had puzzled over since he was little, finally made sense. "I wish I had that sort of courage, Davey. It would have been a whole different life for me if I did, but I could never be that brave." The courage his grandfather was talking about had nothing to do with the war or being a soldier. He was talking about Harry. With his teeth tight together, David sucked in a slow stream of air. His head reeled with a dozen different memories, but he pushed them aside and kept reading.

There's something else, Harry. I never thought I would ever say this, but I'm getting married. I don't want to, Harry, but I think I must.

You know that I've found good work at the Irish pub in Cabbagetown. The owner of the pub (he calls himself the landlord) gave me the job because I'd fought overseas — Niall sent and lost three sons to that bloody war. What I haven't told you before is that this same landlord has a daughter. An old maid. Thirty-four and still unmarried. If you saw her, you'd think that very odd because she's beautiful. Beautiful, but very troubled. I think it would be fair to say Maeve is battling a world of demons, and her father, Niall, is old and worried about her future. He wants to know she'll be taken care of. Not financially — Niall has the pub, and some savings and Maeve will inherit it all. He wants to know that someone will be there to watch out for her when she has one of her spells. That's where I come in.

Niall and I have become friends. He realized

almost from the start that I was . . . different. But despite that, Niall still thinks of me as a son, and he proposed this marriage to protect both Maeve and me. And I love her too, in my way. Nothing is ever straightforward, is it? You know the realities of the world, Harry. It's dangerous for men like us. There isn't a day goes by where I don't find myself dreaming of a life with you, but as long as the law says our love is a crime, I don't see how we can. I don't want to go to jail, and I'm guessing you don't either.

"Grandad was gay," David said aloud. "He was gay with Harry."

David's thoughts flicked to yesterday, when those five police cars zoomed past him on Yonge Street. That's what the protest was about, David remembered. Kelch had been angry at the protesters and had said, "They should have all stayed in their damn closets." That wasn't all, David realized. When Kelch had asked David's mother, "Do you want David to turn out like his grandfather?" what he'd really meant was, do you want David to be gay too?

David stared at the letter and shook his head. "If everyone knew about Grandad, how come nobody told me? I mean, it's not a crime. It's not like they send you to jail for that anymore."

David read on.

I hate breaking my promise to you, Harry — our promises to each other — but there is one thing I can still do for you. I know you have come to love Scotch Gully, and I want to make sure you have a home there for as long as you like. So today, I went to the lawyer's to make my will.

I'm leaving everything to Susan. She's not named in the will — the lawyer knows I will be getting married, and he insisted my will make provisions for future children. I didn't argue. But I asked him to include something that said you may stay on at the farm as long as you wish. He insisted the will wasn't the right place for that. He had all sorts of reasons why it was a bad idea. In the end, I gave in, even though I didn't truly understand his reasons. Instead, he dictated something that says you can stay there until Susan is an adult and can make decisions for herself. It's the last page of this letter.

So stay, Harry. Please. You've never had a home before and if I can't give you what you really want, what I wish for too, for us to be together, at least I can give you this. I'm hoping with all my heart that my family farm will be the home you never had, and you will choose to live out your days there. Who knows, maybe things will change, and the world will accept us. For now, I have to trust that by the time Susan inherits the farm, you will have become like the father she never had, and she will want you to stay.

The letter went on, but David stopped reading. He had questions about his grandfather's other daughter, Susan, but that did not fill his thoughts as much as learning that his grandfather had loved Harry. And not the way you love a best friend or the army buddy who saved your life.

His grandfather loved Harry the way Han Solo loved Princess Leia.

David folded the letter and, with shaking hands, slipped it back inside its envelope. He had to take it now — not just the one page that said Harry could stay, but the whole thing. There would be hell to pay, David knew, but there was no way that he could leave this letter with Kelch. Not when he knew how Kelch felt about people like his grandfather.

"I wish you'd told me yourself, Grandad," David whispered. "But this doesn't change how I feel about you. You were my best friend and my favourite person in the world." With tears in his eyes, he looked up and whispered, "I still love you."

David picked up the letter and headed for the back stairs. If he hurried, he could still make it to 7-Eleven, mail Harry's letter and be back before his mom and Kelch got home from their fancy dinner.

* * * *

He was too late.

When David stepped through the office door,

Kelch was standing there glaring, his face turning darker and darker shades of eggplant-purple with each second. In a blink, he grabbed the letter from David's hand.

"Give it back!" David cried.

Kelch glared at him, ripped the letter in two and shoved the pieces into his pocket. Then he grabbed David's arm.

David tried to wrench free, but Kelch had a vise-like grip on his arm and was squeezing hard.

"Ouch. Stop!" David yelled. "You're hurting me." He called for his mother. Seconds later, David heard her on the steps.

Kelch heard her too. He gave David's arm a last painful squeeze, then let go, smacking David on the back of his head and pushing him forward, toward the back door. Stumbling, arm throbbing and eyes blurry from tears, David ran. Behind him, he heard Kelch's office door slam. When David opened the back door, his mother was there.

"David, what are you doing down here?" she asked.

"Mom, he's got Harry's letter!"

She looked confused. Like she hadn't heard him correctly. Just then, Kelch stuck his head out of his office.

"David says you have Harry's letter, Cameron."

"He's lying. I'll tell you what really happened.

While you and I were out having a special night, the boy snuck downstairs and . . . and he trashed my office."

"What? Wait, I'm coming to see."

She took a step forward, but Kelch barked, "No!"

"I want to see for myself, Cameron," she said.

"Take the boy upstairs, Carla, before I do or say something I'm going to regret."

"It's not fair. I didn't do anything!" David protested. Then he remembered the china flower basket and broken rose, and he sagged. He hadn't "trashed" Kelch's office, but he had broken something, and his mother saw that guilt written across his face plain as day.

"Upstairs. Now," she ordered. Hand on his shoulder, she marched David to his room. Before closing the door, she shook her head and said, "I don't know what to do with you anymore."

"But, Mom, Kelch really does have Harry's letter, the one from Grandad. He ripped it in two and stuck it in his jacket. I saw him do it!"

"Is that another lie, David?" Her disappointment in him hurt far worse than her anger.

"He has the letter, Mom. I swear he does."

She shook her head again. "This was supposed to be a special night," she said and stuck out her hand. There was a diamond ring on her finger. "Cameron asked me to marry him tonight."

"No!" David cried. "You didn't say yes, did you?"

"Of course I did, David. Now go to bed. I'll speak to you in the morning once we've all cooled off."

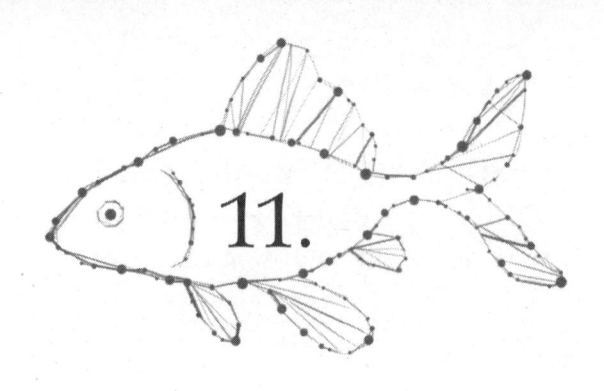

11.

Lizzie

After David called, I worked on my family tree poster then went to bed, but I couldn't sleep. I lay awake worrying about Harry and what would happen if David couldn't find that letter. Where would Harry go, and how would he live? Would he have to get a job? Harry's old, older than my grandma. He's only ever been a soldier and a farmer. Could he even get a job? He could always live with us, I knew that, but would Harry want to stay in Scotch Gully and wake up each morning to see his beautiful farm gone, replaced by a hundred houses? I had so many questions and so few answers. And not just about Harry either. There was also something my grandma said earlier that was making my brain itch.

If Grandma didn't meet Grandfather Ross until the middle of September, how could my mom have been born fat, pink and healthy on April 1st?

The answer is she couldn't. She may have married Grandfather Ross in some great romantic flurry ten days after they met in Vancouver, just like she said, but I'd bet the moon that Phillip Ross was not Mom's father. He couldn't be. The more I thought about that, the madder I got. I was mad at Grandma for not being honest, and I was mad at myself for not figuring it out before. All the clues had been there staring me in the face, and I'd missed every single one.

Take David. The first thing I'd noticed about David when I saw him was that he had bright orange hair just like my mom, and a face with more freckles than skin. That was also just like my mom. And when Harry saw David, he'd said it was like seeing Archie Macrath come back to life.

It should have been obvious then. It was like those whatchamacallits, those transitive law problems they made us do in math class. If David looks like his grandfather and my mom looks like David, then my mom must also look like David's grandfather. The moon had travelled from one side of my bedroom window to the other before I let myself believe what I should have seen from the start: Archie Macrath was my mom's birth father.

Which made him my grandfather.

Which made David my cousin!

Happy as that made me — and it made me over-the-moon happy — my thoughts were still muddled. And not just because my grandmother had lied to Mom and me. Harry must have known too, or at least guessed. Harry and Archie Macrath were best friends; so were Harry and Grandma, and Harry had known my mom most of her life. So even if no one had told him straight out, he had to have seen the resemblance and wondered. With all those clues staring him in the face for all those years, he didn't need to be Sherlock Holmes to have figured it out.

So why didn't he say anything? Was Harry helping Grandma keep it secret? If so, why?

Trying to figure it all out kept me awake until the birds started singing their dawn chorus and Grandma was in the kitchen making oatmeal.

"Lizzie Ross. Hurry up and get out here for breakfast lickety-split, or you'll miss the school bus," Grandma called.

"Coming," I called back. When I got to the kitchen, Grandma was spooning oatmeal into my bowl. She slid the milk and the brown sugar toward me and asked, "Who called last night? You never said."

"David Macrath," I answered.

Grandma's eyebrows lifted high, and her eyes went so wide-open and round that she looked like a great grey owl. "And why was that boy calling you?"

"Because of Harry's letter. The one from David's grandfather?"

"Explain, young lady."

"We couldn't find it yesterday, remember? I think Kelch took the letter while the rest of us were helping the ewe and lamb. David thinks so too. He even promised to look for it."

"And why would that young man help Harry?" Grandma asked. "Wouldn't that mean his mother couldn't take over the farm like she's planning to?"

"He's doing it because Harry saved Grandad's life."

My grandma got owl-faced again. "I beg your pardon? Did you say *Grandad*?"

I must have blushed a million shades of pink right then. I was already thinking of Archie Macrath as my grandfather, but I wasn't ready to talk to Grandma about what I'd figured out. She might change her story. She could claim she misspoke last night. Or maybe she'd pretend that I'd heard things wrong and that of course, she had left Scotch Gully in July. I had to figure a few things out before I confronted her, so I made an excuse.

"I must be tired. I didn't sleep much worrying about Harry. I meant David's grandad, of course," I said, then turned all my attention to my oatmeal.

* * * *

I was a kid on a mission. I had questions, and I figured Miss Gambacort, my social studies teacher, might know where to find the answers. Lunch was the best time to catch her alone. She'd be in either her classroom or the staff room.

The bell rang, and kids poured into the halls carrying their lunch bags. Everyone headed for the lunchroom, which was just the school gym with tables set up inside — Scotch Gully K-8 wasn't big enough to have its very own lunchroom. To get to Miss G's class, I had to go in the opposite direction of the rush, away from the gym and against the current, like a steelhead swimming upstream in fall.

I felt a pinch of guilt asking my teacher for help. Grandma always says that family business is nobody's business but our own, but Grandma says a lot of things, and it turns out not all of the things she says are true.

I needed to talk to Miss G because I wanted to find out more about Grandfather Ross. If I could prove that he shipped out to fight in September and not July like Grandma had been saying my whole life, I would have the proof I needed. Grandma wouldn't be able to change her story then. I also figured that if anyone had that information, it would be the Armed Forces. They have to keep records about everyone, but it's not like you could look up Army or Air Force in our skinny Scotch Gully phone book. And I sure as heck couldn't go to the library and ask for help. That's where my grandma worked. But Miss G was from the city, and she was really big on history and research and stuff. I was betting that she'd know what to do.

I knocked on her classroom door.

"Lizzie Ross," Miss G said. She had a Tupperware container open on her desk, and she was reading a book. "Why aren't you at lunch?"

"Sorry to interrupt. I have a question about our family tree project."

She put down her fork and her book and waved me in. I didn't bother closing the door. The halls were empty because everyone was in the gym eating.

"It must be quite important if it couldn't keep until class," she said.

"It is."

"All right, then. What's your question, Lizzie?"

I took a deep breath and told her everything. Well, mostly everything. I left out my suspicions about who my grandfather really was. But I did explain how I couldn't do my family tree the way she wanted me to, on account of my dad running away to Amsterdam without marrying my mom. And because of that, all I have for my poster is my mom's half of the family tree. I couldn't tell by her face if she was surprised or not. Part of me thought she could be — she's new this year and might not have heard about us yet. But the other part of me knew Scotch Gully was a really small place, and while that's a good thing most times because it means folks look after each other, it also means we all know each other's business.

Then I told her about Grandfather Ross and how even the one measly half of my family tree that I did have was missing a huge branch because I couldn't find any information about him either.

"I see," she said when I was done explaining. "Lizzie, are you asking my permission to skip doing the poster?"

"No, ma'am," I said, shaking my head, even though it was true that when she first assigned the project, all I wanted to do was climb into the barn loft and hide under a bale of hay until school was over. I took a deep breath and explained Harry's misdirection idea, and my plan to make doors in my poster with stories inside each one.

"Lizzie, I think that's brilliant," she said. "I am so impressed."

"Thanks, Miss Gambacort. The thing is, since all I know about my dad is his name, and since Grandfather Ross was killed in the war, my poster's pretty empty."

"Do you have any pictures of them that you could use?"

I shake my head again.

"How do you think I can help you, Lizzie?"

"Well, Grandfather Ross was in the Air Force.

His plane was shot down over Italy. You know tons about World War II. You've taught us a bunch already. So . . ."

"So?"

I shrugged my shoulders as my face flushed pink. Maybe this was a dumb idea.

"It's okay, Lizzie. Keep going. I'm curious to understand your logic."

I took a breath for courage. "Well, I figure the Armed Forces must have some record of my grandfather. Something that would say his date and place of birth, when and where he signed up, and the date his unit shipped out. Since he died fighting overseas, I figure they must have a record of that too."

"Lizzie, that's brilliant! I am so proud of you. They absolutely would have that information. I would love to see your grandmother's face when you show her what you've found."

Miss G thought she was helping me do something kind for my family. It felt kind of rotten, not telling her the real reason. But I told myself it was more important to find out the truth. Hiding the real reason that I wanted the information was a necessary misdirection.

"The problem is, Miss Gambacort," I said, "I don't know how to reach the Armed Forces or how to ask them for the information."

Miss G stood up so quickly the backs of her

knees snapped against her chair, knocking it backward.

She walked around her desk toward me and grabbed my hand.

"As it happens," she said, "I know just who to ask. Come with me."

Miss G had long legs, and she walked fast. I almost had to run to keep up with her. In no time, we were outside Principal Fleming's office and she was knocking on his door. Quick, excited knocks.

Mr. Fleming looked even older than Harry. He had a huge forehead with white, shaggy, Albert Einstein eyebrows that stuck out in all directions. His hair was white too, and thick as a horse's mane, but he wore it slicked back from his forehead, every hair glued in place. When I'd first started school, I asked Grandma how Principal Fleming's hair could stay wet all day. She'd chuckled and told me, "It's not wet, Lizzie. That shine comes from wearing too much Brylcreem. It was all the rage back in the forties. There was even a squadron of fliers in the Royal Air Force who called themselves the Brylcreem Boys. Back then, boys wore so much goop on their hair that I swear, if you stood beside one on a sunny day, you'd need sunglasses just to keep the glare out of your eyes."

"Come in," Mr. Fleming called through the door.

Inside, I tried not to look at Principal Fleming's

hair, but his office had fluorescent lights in the ceiling that bounced off the goop in his hair, making his head shinier than ever. It drew my eyes like a porch light draws a moth.

"What have we here? You're not in some sort of trouble, are you, Miss Ross?"

"Not at all, Malcom," Miss G answered.

I shook my head.

"Well, that's good, because I have high hopes for young Lizzie. I taught her mother years ago. Wonderful student, Susan Ross. She was one of the few girls in her class who headed off to university. She's a lawyer now, you know?"

"I didn't know that Malcolm, but I'd wager that young Lizzie here is going to make us equally proud."

Miss G explained what I was looking for and why. The way she explained things made it sound like I was a cross between a social studies protegé and the world's most thoughtful granddaughter. I looked down at my hands so I didn't have to look either one of them in the eye.

"Malcolm, you served in the war," Miss G said. "If I remember correctly, you're still very involved with the Armed Forces."

"I'm flattered that you listened to all my boring stories, Terry. And yes, as it happens, I do have several connections. In fact, my old platoon-mate stayed in the service and now runs the entire records department. I am sure he'll be able to help us." Principal Fleming turned his attention to me. "This is a very fine thing you're doing for your grandmother, Miss Ross."

I swallowed hard while he reached across his desk for the Rolodex, spinning it around until he found the card he was looking for.

"Before I call Lieutenant-Colonel Degenhart, you'll need to tell me everything you know about your grandfather so we can help narrow the search."

I pushed my guilt down as deeply as I could. "His name was Phillip Ross."

Principal Fleming wrote that down. Truth or lies, I tried to think of everything Grandma had ever told me.

"He wasn't born in Canada," I said. "He was from Scotland. He came to Canada just before we declared war on Germany. So . . . before 1939."

Miss G patted my shoulder, and I looked up at her. She was beaming at me, proud that I remembered dates from class, I guess. I felt kind of queasy, but I managed a mouth-smile back at her.

"Anything else?" Mr. Fleming asked.

"He lived in Vancouver — that's where my grandmother met him — and he flew planes. Well, maybe he just flew in the planes. I don't know if he was a pilot, a navigator or something else."

"In planes, you say. That would put him in the RCAF. Royal Canadian Air Force. That's a very helpful detail, Miss Ross. That will narrow the search immensely. Do you know his squadron number?"

I shook my head. "Sorry."

"That's fine," he said. "Are there any other details you can remember?"

"My grandmother said they married in Vancouver in July 1940, and he was shipped out soon after. I don't have the date, but he was already overseas when my mom was born on April 1st, 1941. My grandfather died when his plane got shot down over Italy in 1944 or 1945. I'm not sure exactly when, but my mom was already back in Scotch Gully when she started kindergarten."

Principal Fleming's forehead wrinkled. "Shot down over Italy, you say?"

"Yes, sir."

"1945?"

"Maybe 1944?"

"I see. Let me call my friend." Principal Fleming picked up the phone and dialed.

There was a lot of small talk, the kind Grandma has when she sees someone in town that she hasn't seen in a while. Talk about aches and pains, children and grandchildren, animals and crops, and lots of talk about the weather. Then Mr. Fleming explained my story and gave his old friend my grandfather's name (Phillip Ross), where he'd lived (Vancouver), where and when he died (Italy), and that he was in the RCAF.

"I thought as much," Principal Fleming said. "Will you hold one moment, Gerald?" Principal Fleming asked me, "Miss Ross, are you certain your grandfather's plane went down over Italy?"

"Yes, sir."

"And he enlisted in Vancouver?"

"Yes, sir. My mom's birth certificate says Vancouver. We're doing a family tree in class, so I've looked at all the birth certificates from that side of our family, right back to my great-great-great-grandfather's."

Miss G gave my shoulder another squeeze. Principal Fleming's forehead wrinkled so much that his eyebrows knit together like one big handlebar mustache hanging above his eyes.

He spoke into the receiver. "Did you hear that, Gerald?" Then his face got cloudy. "I see. Could you check if you have any Phillip Rosses from British Columbia in any branch of the service? I'll hold."

Any?

Principal Fleming explained. "There were no airborne divisions from Vancouver that flew missions over Italy. Some flew in the Pacific theatre, and the 405 went across to Germany, but none of those were involved in the Italian theatre."

"What does that mean?" I asked.

"I suppose it means that either you're missing some important parts of your grandfather's story or you've mixed them up somehow."

I felt Miss G's hand squeeze my shoulder again. This time it wasn't because she was proud of me. It was because she felt sorry for me. Principal Fleming looked like he felt sorry for me too. I pressed my lips together tight to stop myself from smiling.

Finally, his friend came back on the line. I couldn't hear what they said, but I heard the hum of a conversation, then Principal Fleming hung up.

"Lieutenant-Colonel Degenhart can't find any record of your grandfather in the RCAF. His files show six men out of British Columbia named Phillip Ross, but they were army, and all of those six men were born here in Canada. I'm sorry, young lady. Perhaps we could narrow it down further if we had a middle name. Why don't you ask your grandmother?"

"I can't."

"It's true that it won't be the nice surprise for your grandmother that you hoped for, Lizzie." Principal Fleming called me by my first name instead of calling me "young lady" or "Miss Ross"; he was feeling sorry for me. "But your grandmother will still appreciate what you're doing for her. And when you have more information, we can try again."

I stared down at my hands once again. They were trembling. Miss G saw it too because she wrapped her arm across my shoulders.

I expect she thought that I was shaking because I was so disappointed.

But I wasn't disappointed at all.

I was trembling because I'd figured it out.

I'd been trying to prove that Phillip Ross shipped out to fight in September and not July. Instead, I'd learned that there was no Phillip Ross.

Phillip Ross did not exist.

Grandma made him up.

I just didn't know why.

12.

David

David sat on his bed, back against the wall, with his sweatshirt hood pulled down low over his forehead. It was noon, and that meant any minute now he would hear his mother's heels click-clacking up the stairs. Sure enough, before his clock said 12:02, she was standing in his doorway. She must set an alarm, he grumbled.

"We're swamped downstairs," his mother announced, "so I can't stay long, but, David, we need to talk about last night."

He'd been expecting a lecture since his latest run-in with Kelch, but his mother had been eerily silent.

"Yeah?" he answered. He knew it sounded smart-alecky, but David was angry. Angry that Kelch stole Harry's letter, twice — once from the farm, and once right out of David's hand — and had ripped it in half. He was angry that Kelch lied, and angry that his mother believed Kelch and not him. How could she *ever* agree to marry somebody like that?

Either his mother hadn't noticed David's attitude, or she chose to ignore it. "I called your school this morning," she said. "You'll be happy to know that the janitor fetched your backpack down from the basketball net. Your action figures are still inside."

David *was* happy about that, but he also knew that her good news was the spoonful of sugar for the medicine that was yet to come.

"I'm worried about you, David," she said. "You're turning into someone I barely recognize. Maybe Cameron is right. Maybe Rosehill Public School isn't the best place for you."

There it was, the bad news. David dragged himself to the edge of the bed, swung his legs over the side, and pushed his sweatshirt hood back. "Mom, please, don't send me away to school."

His mother had dark circles under eyes, and her forehead was creased with worry wrinkles. "You should never have gone into Cameron's office. Whatever possessed you to do that?"

"I had to get Harry's letter back."

"Oh, David," she said, shaking her head.

"But it's true, Mom. Kelch took the letter."

"Don't call him that, David."

"What? Kelch? What do you want me to call him?"

"Well . . ."

"No. Nuh-uh," David said, folding his arms across his chest and shaking his head. "I don't care if you *are* going to marry him. I'm not going to call him Dad. Not ever."

They had reached an impasse. For David, it wasn't just that his mother had inserted Kelch into their lives. David was hurt and angry that she had believed and sided with Kelch. His mother, seeing everything that David had done since Monday — the fight at school, the damage Kelch claimed David had done in the office — was worried that Kelch may be right, and David was headed down a dark path toward a troubled future. Something had to change.

"David," she said, "I'm going to ask you a question, and I need you to tell me the truth. Will you do that?"

He nodded.

"Did you break something in Cameron's office?"

He hesitated.

"Don't lie to me, David," she warned.

"It was an accident, Mom," he blurted. "I was reaching for Grandad's will and knocked the china flower basket over. I broke off a flower. But, Mom,

I'll get some of that Krazy Glue they advertise on TV. I'll even buy it with my own money and glue the flower back on so he'll hardly notice."

"That's not what Cameron said."

"What do you mean? What did he say?"

"He said you knew those flowers used to belong to his mother, and you smashed them deliberately. To hurt him."

"What?"

"It's not just one rose that broke off, David. The thing's been shattered into dozens of pieces. It can't be repaired."

"I didn't do *that*!" David protested.

"I saw the bits in his garbage myself. Along with all the boarding school brochures you ripped up."

"Not me!"

"Then who?" she asked. Disappointment oozed from her.

David remembered the boarding school application, filled out and sitting under the china flower basket.

"Kelch. He did it himself. He's trying to make me look bad so you'll agree to send me away."

"Don't be ridiculous, David."

Downstairs in Rosehill Realty, the phones were ringing.

"I have to go."

"If you send me to boarding school, I'll . . ."

David was near tears. "I'll run away. I will! I'd rather live under a bridge or in a barn."

With tears in her own eyes, his mother said, "Please, David. We can't go on like this."

David heard heavy footsteps take the stairs two at a time. Kelch appeared.

"Carla, you need to get downstairs," he said in an angry whisper.

"Just one minute, Cameron."

"Now! I've got an office full of realtors *trying* to talk to clients, and that damn phone keeps ringing." As if on cue, the phone rang again. "Oh, for crying out loud," Kelch said and headed downstairs.

"I have to go, David. We'll talk later."

"At lunch?"

"Not today. There's leftover pizza in the fridge. That will have to do. Make sure you have a glass of milk too."

"But . . ."

"Cameron will be going to your grandfather's farm later this afternoon to talk to Mr. Doak. I would have liked to go with him, but now I think I'd better stay here. I don't think I can trust you enough to stay here alone."

"Kelch is going to the farm to give Harry an eviction notice, isn't he?"

She raised her eyebrows.

"I saw it on his desk last night."

"Then I guess you have all the answers now, don't you?" She turned and headed for the stairs.

"Did you move us out of Grandad's house because he was gay?" David called after her.

His mother froze, went rigid. She stopped, turned around.

"Kelch thinks being gay is bad, doesn't he? That's why he didn't like Grandad."

His mother opened her mouth as if to speak, but no words came out.

"I'm right, aren't I?" David exclaimed. "I'll tell you something else I'm right about, Mom. Being gay's not bad, and it's not against the law. Not anymore. Everybody knows that." He pressed his lips together for a moment, then expelled an angry burst of air. "That protest on Yonge Street yesterday — the one Kelch called the police about — we should have been there, Mom. We should have marched for Grandad. You've got to stand up for what's right. You've got to stand up to bullies. You did when they wanted to kick you out of school for being pregnant with me. Grandad supported you then, right? And he supported you when you didn't want to marry my father. Well, Mom, we should have supported Grandad."

"David . . ." It was just one word, his name. Once she'd said it, it hung in the air between them.

David pressed on. "It doesn't matter that Grandad was gay. It doesn't change how I feel. I don't love him any less. Do you?"

His mother flushed pink. "Where is this coming from, David?"

"From Grandad's letter to Harry! I told you! I read it last night before Kelch tore it in half . . ."

His mother's eyes glistened. David thought she might cry. Just then, Kelch reappeared, his face like thunder.

His mother said, "I have to go, David. I'm sorry. But we're going to have a *long* talk about this later. Okay?"

She turned and bolted down the stairs, leaving David alone.

He went to the kitchen to get the pizza out of the fridge and saw his eggs, which made him think about Lizzie, which made him think about Harry. David really wanted to see Harry again. He had so many questions about his grandfather. Especially now. David stood there, eating a cold slice of pizza, when an idea hit him. An idea so crazy, he thought it just might work. *When Kelch drives to Harry's this afternoon*, David decided, *I'm going with him. He just won't know it.*

David's heart was racing as he slipped on his sneakers, still damp from being washed yesterday. He found a piece of paper and hurriedly wrote a note.

Mom, I swear I didn't do those all things Kelch said. I did break a flower, but just one, and that was an accident. I didn't do any of that other stuff. He's lying. And, Mom, there really was a letter, and it said Harry could stay at the farm. It said something else too, but you left before I got a chance to tell you. Grandad had another kid. Her name was Susan, and she was seven years old when Grandad wrote his will. Kelch lied about that too, remember? I can't stop you from marrying him, but I have to try and help Harry. That's what Grandad would have wanted.

David

P.S. I've gone to the farm.

David left the note on his pillow, then snuck down the back stairs, ninja-style, careful not to let the stairs creak. Heart racing, he ran across the small parking lot to the far side of Kelch's car and opened the passenger door. The trunk lever was a yellow button inside the glove compartment. He pushed it, then pushed the door firmly but quietly closed.

Big as the trunk was, there wasn't a lot of free space inside. David climbed in, found a handhold inside the trunk roof and yanked it just enough to engage the pull-down motor. Once he heard it start, he ducked down fast, then scrabbled over a stack of For Sale signs to the deepest part of the trunk. He curled up, head on his arm, and settled in to wait for Kelch.

This is either the bravest or the dumbest thing I've ever done, he thought.

But he didn't have time to dwell on that. The driver's door soon opened, then shut, and seconds later, the large motor growled to life. After that, things got uncomfortable fast.

There were a lot of street lights on Yonge Street. Every time Kelch braked, David was flung forward. When Kelch hit the gas, David rolled backward into the stack of sharp-edged For Sale signs. Between all the stopping and going, he was so busy rolling around that he didn't have much time to think. That may have been a good thing, because once they reached the highway and things got smooth, David started to worry about everything he hadn't thought of before.

Like . . .

Would he run out of air?

And . . .

Would the car exhaust leak inside the trunk and kill him?

Once his imagination kicked in, David started to panic. He thought about everything that could go wrong. His breathing became small and fast, which made him think maybe he *was* running out of air, which made him breathe even smaller and faster.

Finally, the car slowed right down and turned left, and the road became bumpy. He heard the distinct sound of gravel crunching beneath car tires. The car stopped, the engine turned off and David heard a dog bark. Expo! He'd made it. They were at the farm.

As soon as David heard the driver's door open and slam shut, he scrabbled over the For Sale signs. He expected that Kelch would head straight for the farmhouse to deliver the eviction notice and that, David decided, would be the perfect time to sneak out of the trunk. He'd hide in the barn, and then, once Kelch had gone, David would find Harry and tell him about the letter and the will.

David felt around in the dark for a button or a lever that would open the trunk.

Nothing.

I'm an idiot. I should have made sure I could get out before I got in.

Then, over the pounding of his heart, he heard a woman's voice. It sounded familiar, though echoey and a little muffled.

"Can I help you?" she said.

"Good morning, ma'am. I'm here to see Harry Doak." That was Kelch.

David was surprised that he could hear them so well. It sounded like they were talking into a tin-can telephone, but their words were clear enough.

"Mr. Doak is busy," the woman answered. "And you are?"

"My name is Cameron Kelch, ma'am. I'm the proprietor of Rosehill Realty." Kelch was trying to sound all sugar and sweetness, but David knew it was a fake sweet. Like the powder in those pink paper packages his mother put in her coffee instead of sugar.

"You must be that real estate person who's been threatening Harry. My granddaughter told me all about you."

Granddaughter? This was Lizzie's grandma! He thought he recognized her voice. He'd heard her briefly last night when he was talking to Lizzie on the phone. David redoubled his efforts to locate a latch that would open the trunk from the inside.

"What's that in your hand?" Lizzie's grandmother asked. "Is that Harry's letter? My granddaughter thought you stole it. It seems she was right."

"This?" Kelch said. "No. Of course not! I would never do that."

"Liar!" David cried. He didn't have time to search for a trunk release; he had to tell Lizzie's grandmother what really happened. He had to tell her what was in that envelope. He had to get out right now! He banged on the trunk roof with both fists.

"Help, help. Let me out," he yelled. Expo barked.

"What on earth? There's someone in there!" Lizzie's grandmother cried. "Mr. Kelch, you open that trunk this minute!"

The trunk opened, and daylight flooded in. David had to squint his eyes almost shut. Kelch appeared first as a giant-headed silhouette, but Lizzie's grandma quickly pushed in front of him. As soon as she saw David, one hand flew to her mouth. The other hand went over her heart.

"Dear Lord," she said. "You look just like him. You are the very spitting image of Archie Macrath. Here, let me help," she said, and put her hand out.

"You're Lizzie's grandmother, aren't you?" David said.

She nodded. "David, isn't it?"

"Yes, ma'am." He tried to grab her hand, but he was stuck. His sweatshirt was snagged on the corner of a For Sale sign. He tugged and tugged, but it wouldn't pull free, so he unzipped it and shrugged it off, first one arm then the other. Then he climbed out of the trunk. Expo nuzzled his leg.

"What on earth happened there?" Lizzie's grandmother asked, pointing at his arm. "What are those bruises from?"

David looked at Kelch.

"He must have bumped against something in the trunk," Kelch said.

"Rubbish," said Lizzie's grandmother. "Those bruises are not new. Look at the colour." In the space of a heartbeat, Lizzie's grandmother had her arm wrapped around David. "It's clear your mother doesn't know where you are, David," she said. "The first thing we're going to have to do is call her."

"There's no need for that," Kelch said. "I'll be done with Mr. Doak in a few minutes, then I'll take David home."

Kelch sounded polite, respectable, but David could tell that inside, Kelch was like a hand grenade with the pin pulled. Kelch reached for David's wrist to pull him back inside the car. David figured it was all over then. He'd never get to see Harry now. Never get to tell him what he knew. Never get to ask Harry about his grandad.

Whack!

Fast as a bullwhip Lizzie's grandmother slapped Kelch's hand. Kelch yanked it back like he'd touched a hot element on the stove.

"You are not taking this child anywhere until I clear it with his mother, do you hear me?" she said.

"I am engaged to his mother." Kelch was indignant; he was unused to people not doing what he said. "I'm going to be the boy's stepfather."

"Engaged isn't married," said Lizzie's grandmother, and she put herself firmly between David and Kelch even though she was old and small and Kelch towered over her. David's chest swelled with admiration as he watched the standoff. Kelch could have just picked her up and moved her out of the way, but Lizzie's grandmother looked so fierce and ready to fight that Kelch did nothing. David thought she was like Luke Skywalker facing down a line of AT-AT walkers.

"Get. In. The. Car. David," Kelch growled.

David looked at Kelch, then he looked at Lizzie's grandmother. He made a choice.

"No. I'm staying here."

Kelch turned purple. There was no going back now, David knew. Even if he wanted to.

"Fine," Kelch said and turned to Lizzie's grandmother. "Go ahead. Call his mother. She'll side with me. She'll insist you turn him over to me. In the meantime, I need to find Mr. Doak. Where is he?"

"Mr. Doak is busy with the ewes."

"Is the lamb okay?" David asked. "And the ewe?" Despite everything that was happening around him, David had a personal stake in those animals.

Lizzie's grandma smiled, and even if she hadn't been as brave as Luke Skywalker just moments ago, David would have decided right then and there that he liked her. Her smile reminded him of Lizzie, warm and sunny, and full of good intention.

"Both mother and lamb are doing well, thanks to you."

"Lizzie too," David reminded her.

Kelch grew impatient with the chit-chat. He thrust the envelope at Lizzie's grandmother. She reached for it.

"No!" David yelled. "Don't take it! It's an eviction notice for Harry." He pointed at Kelch. "And he does too have Harry's letter. Or he did," David corrected himself. "He ripped it up last night. I saw him do it!"

Kelch shot daggers at him. David was certain that if Lizzie's grandmother hadn't been there, Kelch would have done worse than squeeze his arm or cuff him on the back of the head again.

But Kelch did none of those things. He collected himself, turned to Lizzie's grandmother and said, "You can't believe a word this boy says."

Lizzie's grandmother crossed her arms across her chest.

"I'm quite serious," said Kelch. He was scarily calm. "Did you know he's been suspended from school for attacking a classmate so severely that the boy had to go to the hospital?"

For the first time, David understood what it meant when someone said they felt the rug being pulled out from under them. Until that moment, David thought Lizzie's grandmother believed him. But now . . . she looked at David, sized him up. David felt sure she believed Kelch.

"Ah, now you see, don't you?" said Kelch. "He's not the fine young man you think he is. It gets worse. Last night, petulant and angry about my engagement to his mother, this boy broke into my office and trashed it."

Kelch was making him sound like a juvenile delinquent, someone who belonged in a reform school. David felt stomach-churningly sick.

"Did you go into this man's office last night, David?" Lizzie's grandmother asked him.

He couldn't lie. "I did. But only to get Harry's letter back. I didn't trash anything."

Lizzie's grandmother stared hard at David. He couldn't read her face, but no grown-up had believed him, not since his grandad died, so why should Lizzie's grandmother be any different? It was hopeless. She'd send him back with Kelch, for sure.

Lizzie's grandmother turned from David to Kelch and said, "I think it's crystal clear, Mr. Kelch."

Here it comes, thought David.

"You, sir," she continued, "are both a thief *and* a liar. You can take your eviction notice and your big fancy car and head right back to the city."

Lizzie's grandmother believed him! David was over the moon!

"I'm taking the boy," Kelch said and took a threatening step toward them. Expo growled.

"Think very hard about what you do next,

Mr. Kelch. My daughter is out back. She's a lawyer and knows how to deal with the likes of you." Then Lizzie's grandmother took David's hand and pulled him toward the porch steps.

Kelch started to follow. "I can't leave without the boy. His mother would—"

"You set even one foot on this porch, and I'll be calling Constable Washburn."

Kelch bristled. "May I remind you, madam, that this isn't your property."

"It isn't yours either, is it?"

"I am engaged to the owner."

"Engaged isn't married, remember? And you mind this . . . I've known our Constable Washburn since he was in short pants. If it's a contest between your word and mine, who do you think he's going to believe? Some puffed-up stranger from the city, or the woman who used to read *McElligot's Pool* to him every week during library storytime? Especially once he sees the bruises on this child's arm."

Lizzie's grandma did not wait around for Kelch's answer. With David's hand in hers, they were through the door and into the kitchen in no time. She stood at the screen door, hands on her hips, glaring at Kelch like she was daring him to come closer. Then she turned to David. "That's one problem taken care of. Now, let's tackle the next one. Let's call your mother. She must be beside herself with worry! What's her number?"

At Rosehill Realty, the answering machine picked up.

"That's weird. I guess she's busy?" David said.

"You don't sound too sure."

"Well, she might have gone upstairs to check on me," David admitted. "But I left a note."

"Then we'll wait for a few minutes and try her office again. In the meantime, I've a job for you. My daughter is out back with Harry and the new lamb. Run and fetch her."

David nodded, eager to help.

"And, David, don't forget to tell her about seeing that letter. That's important."

"But Kelch ripped it up," David said. "It's gone."

"It still matters," she said.

David wasn't sure how, but he nodded and headed out the kitchen door at a run.

When he got to the birthing pen, he didn't see Lizzie's mom, but Harry was there.

"David," Harry said. "What on earth are you doing here?"

David froze. There were so many thoughts swimming in his head right then, all those things his grandfather had written, but only one thing truly mattered. David sprinted the last few metres, threw his arms around Harry and gave him the largest, longest hug.

"David? What is it?"

The whole story tumbled out then. About the stolen letter, about reading it, about David trying to steal it back for Harry and about Kelch ripping it up.

"Please don't be mad at me, Harry. I shouldn't have read it. I know it was private, really private, but, Harry . . ."

"Yes, David?"

"It doesn't change how I feel about Grandad. Not one bit. And . . ." David's cheeks flushed pink. "And now with you, it's like I have another grandfather."

David saw tears in Harry's eyes. "Harry? Are you okay?"

"Of course. Oh, I wish Archie was here to see this. This would have made his heart light. He worried things between you might change if you knew."

"Never," David whispered earnestly.

Harry smiled. Then he pointed to a new lamb inside the pen. "See that, David? That little fellow over there is the ram lamb you helped bring into the world. Would you like to name him?"

"Really?" David said. "What about Lizzie? She's supposed to do that, isn't she?"

"She won't mind a bit. She can name the next one. What do you think, David? Any ideas?"

David did have an idea. A name that Lizzie

would love, because it was funny, like the names she'd picked.

"*Lamb*do Calrissian," David said.

Harry's face puckered in confusion. David laughed.

"It's from *The Empire Strikes Back*. Grandad took me to see the movie four times last year."

"Well, okay then," Harry said. "Would you like to feed Lambdo? Lizzie's mother is getting his bottle ready."

Hearing Harry mention Lizzie's mother reminded David of what he'd been sent to do. "I'm supposed to fetch Lizzie's mom to deal with Kelch. Harry, he brought an eviction notice!"

"Don't fret about that, David," Harry said. "It's enough right now that you're here." Then Harry called, "Susan!"

"Susan?" David said. "Lizzie's mother is Susan? Susan, from the letter?"

Harry nodded.

"Then . . . then she's my aunt! Harry, I have an aunt!" David felt something take hold inside his chest and grow and grow and grow.

"Yes, she is, David," Harry said, putting a hand gently on David's shoulder. "But she doesn't know."

"We need to tell her, Harry!"

"No, David. Her mother has to do that. When she's ready. Do you understand?"

An orange head and a heavily freckled face appeared from the barn, and David saw his aunt for the first time. Lizzie was right. They did look alike. She'd also noticed, he could tell. But before Susan could speak, Harry reminded David of his job.

David nodded. "Your mother sent me to get you," he said. "Kelch is here with an eviction notice for Harry."

"Is that right?" she said. She wiped her hands on her jeans and marched off to deal with Kelch. *Whoa*, David thought, *she's tough. Kelch won't be able to push her around so easily.*

He turned to Harry and whispered, "Harry, we have to tell her."

Harry shook his head.

"But, Harry," said David. "It's important. It's about the farm. It belongs to her too."

"No, David. It used to be that way, but Mr. Kelch said there was a new will that names only your mother."

"That was a lie, Harry! I read Grandad's will last night. It said . . ." David screwed up his face trying to remember the exact wording. "It said *my present and future children*, and it was written *before* my mom was born."

Harry's eyes opened wide. "Are you sure, David?"

David nodded.

"Let's go," Harry said. "Hurry."

He ran with Harry toward the parked cars where Lizzie's mom was facing off against Kelch, but before David had a chance to share what he knew about the will, his mother's car bumped up the drive. Moments later, two people got out. His mother and . . . Lizzie? In his mother's car?

Strange as it was seeing Lizzie with his mother, David didn't have time to wonder how that happened. His mother was marching straight at him. Then, two metres away, she stopped. He thought it was because she was angry and couldn't stand being close to him.

His chin trembled. "Mom?"

"How?" was all she said. Just one word.

"I hid in Kelch's trunk." There was a wobble in his voice.

"Carla," Kelch interrupted. "How did you get here so quickly?"

She didn't answer. She didn't even look at Kelch. She kept staring at David.

"I've been so stupid," she said. "Stupid about everything."

"Yes," Kelch agreed. "David's behaviour *has* deteriorated alarmingly. We can fix this, sweetheart, but we'll have to act quickly. For his sake, and ours."

This whole time his mother's eyes had never left David's face. She stared at him like he was a stranger, someone she didn't recognize, but as Kelch spoke, her attention was drawn ever so slowly away from David.

"You're right, Cameron. I do need to act quickly," she said, and David's stomach tightened. "David said some things today, things he couldn't have known unless . . ."

She reached into her purse and pulled something out. David recognized it immediately. It was Harry's letter, Scotch-taped back together where Kelch had ripped it in two.

"You lied to me, Cameron. You stole this from Harry. David didn't trash your office, did he? It was you. You did it yourself, then blamed a child. Who does that?"

"Carla," Kelch said. His voice was shaky. "Please. You've got to understand. I did it for us. I was protecting our dream."

"That was *your* dream, Cam. I wanted a family. I wanted David to have a mother and a father, like other kids. I thought that would be better for him. Stupid," she said again, shaking her head slowly side to side. "I can't believe I let your poison get so deep inside me."

David's jaw went slack. He could not have looked more surprised if he'd just seen the Loch Ness monster appear in the chicken coop.

Kelch, on the other hand, did not look well. But

David's mother wasn't finished with him quite yet.

"I will hate myself forever for letting you convince me that my father was some . . . some deviant I needed to protect David from," she said. "My father was a good and gentle man, and I abandoned him. He died alone, and I will have to live with that for the rest of my days. But what I will not live with any longer, Cameron Kelch, is you." She slid her engagement ring off her finger and handed it to him. "I'd like you to leave."

For a moment, Kelch seemed to deflate, like a balloon leaking air. But it didn't last. In an eye-blink he puffed up once more and, like the gasbag he was, glared at David as if everything was his fault. Then Kelch turned on his heels, got into his car and drove off.

His mother handed the letter to Harry, saying, "I'm *so* sorry."

"Thank you," Harry said, his voice throaty with emotion.

Then she turned to David and asked, "Will you forgive me?"

"Excuse me. Excuse me!" Lizzie's mother interrupted. "I'm glad you're all happy families now, but I need to know, Ms. Macrath, does this mean you will not be evicting Harry?"

David's mother looked up, and with a cat-that-swallowed-the-cream grin, she said, "Personally, I'd be happy for Harry to stay right where he is for as long as he likes. But you'll have to check with my sister. We own this place together."

"Fine," Lizzie's mother said. "And where do I find her?"

"Well, you won't have to look far," David's mother said, ruffling his hair. "The family resemblance is undeniable."

Lizzie's mother was confused. "Will someone, anyone, please tell me what's going on?"

On the porch, Lizzie's grandmother had been watching the whole scene unfold. "You best come inside," she said. "All of you. I'll make tea." Then she turned and headed into the kitchen.

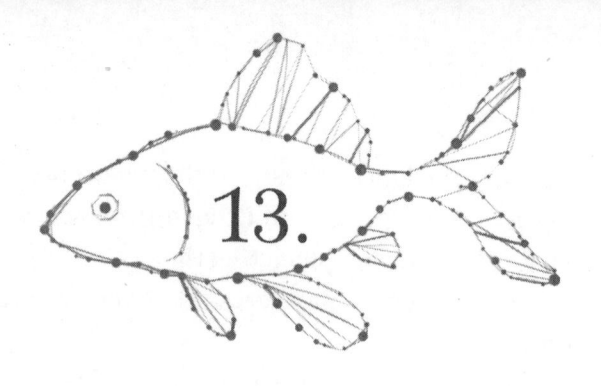

13.

Lizzie

Grandma headed into the kitchen, with Harry hurrying behind like an Olympic race walker. That left me, Mom, David and Aunt Carla standing there facing each other, saying nothing. David and Aunt Carla (I have an aunt!) were all grins, and I wanted to hug them both, but I was too worried about my mom. She stood there stony-faced, looking at each of us. Grandma always said Mom was inscrutable, which just means you can't ever tell what she's thinking. That's part of what makes her a good lawyer, I guess. I'm the opposite of inscrutable. Whatever I'm thinking shows up on my face in big, easy-to-read print, like a picture book. Right then, that book had two illustrations: a happiest-she's-ever-been girl, because her family had just doubled in size, and a scared kid, worried what would happen to her family once all the secrets were revealed.

"Are you coming?" Aunt Carla asked David.

"In a minute, Mom. I want to talk to Lizzie."

She nodded. Once the moms were out of earshot, David turned to me and said, "You know, don't you?"

"That we're cousins? Yeah." I threw my arms around him and gave him the biggest, fiercest hug. He hugged me back just as strongly.

"How did *you* find out?" I asked him.

"It was in my grandad's letter."

"So then everyone knows, except my mom?"

David nodded. Ahead, Mom was walking through the porch door and into the kitchen. I worried about how she'd feel when she learned the truth.

"We better get inside," I said. I linked my arm through his, and together we headed to the porch.

"Hey, Lizzie," he asked. "How the heck did you end up in my mom's car?"

I chuckled. "She didn't give me much choice. She pulled in the driveway just as the school bus dropped me off and pretty much ordered me to get in the car. She was loaded for bear."

"Huh?"

"Spoiling for a fight?"

David chuckled. "That's something else I'm going to have to learn when we move here. You guys talk funny."

I hadn't thought about it before, but I suppose we did.

By the time David and I arrived in the kitchen, Grandma had brewed a large pot of tea and everyone was already seated around the table. Harry was serving up a plate of leftover griddle cakes and zucchini bread.

David pulled up a chair. I put my backpack on the floor and sat down beside him. There was so much tension in that room you could feel the weight of it. Grandma tried to pour tea, but her hand shook.

"Is there something you want to tell me?" Mom asked Grandma.

I'd always figured my grandma was fearless. It never mattered who it was; if she felt someone was on the wrong side of being good and decent, Grandma would always stand up and be counted. Seeing her this nervous was hard.

Grandma looked at Harry. He nodded, then she took a big breath and said, "Archie Macrath was your father, Susan. Carla is your sister. Half-sister."

My mom's face remained unreadable. "Did Phillip Ross know he wasn't my father?" she asked.

"There was no Phillip Ross," I blurted.

Everyone turned to look at me.

"How did you . . . ?" Grandma looked shocked. You could have knocked her over with a feather.

"Explain, Lizzie," my mom said. She sounded

every bit the lawyer right then.

I took a moment to organize my story. I started with finding the photograph of Grandma and Archie Macrath, and finished with the story of how Principal Fleming's army friend couldn't find any records for Phillip Ross.

"But why?" Mom asked Grandma. "Why all the lies?"

"It was 1940, Susan."

"And?"

"The world was a different place then. Forty years ago, when I was pregnant with you . . ." Grandma shook her head, took another deep breath and changed direction. "Before Lizzie was born, when you worked with the CCLA, Susan, did anyone ever bring you a case about the adoption mandate?"

I looked over at my mom. She was shaking her head. "I've never heard of it," she said.

"I shouldn't be surprised, I suppose. It's been the government's dirty secret for years. Like the British home children. Isn't that right, Harry?"

He nodded.

Grandma sighed then continued. "In the 1940s, the government believed they knew best, and they decided that unmarried mothers were not fit to keep their babies."

I could hardly swallow. "Mom wasn't married when she had me."

"Exactly, Lizzie," Grandma said. "But you were born in 1968. It was still happening then, but not nearly as often. Women were beginning to stand up for themselves by then. In 1941 unwed mothers were *expected* to give their babies up for adoption. It was considered the decent thing to do. The government had decided that only nuclear families — homes with a mother and a father — were suitable for raising children. Sometimes they would force a woman to sign away her rights. Sometimes they would browbeat her with talk about her godlessness and immorality until she agreed. And sometimes they simply took the babies and had them adopted out to *proper* families."

"Grandma, is this for real? Did the government really take babies away from their mothers?"

"Yes. Over three hundred thousand."

"So . . . if you hadn't lied and pretended to be married, they could have taken Mom away from you?"

"Right there in the hospital." Grandma turned to look at my mother. "I was desperate to keep you, Susan. I loved you from the moment I knew you were growing inside me. And I loved Archie. I was so certain that when he came back from war, we would marry and be a family.

"So I moved to Vancouver, bought myself a wedding ring, and I lied. I lied to the hospital, to the government and my own parents."

"Then my name is not really Susan Ross. But I'm not a Macrath either. I guess legally I'm a Sinclair. Lizzie too."

Then it hit me. I picked up my backpack and pulled out the old book from the Vancouver library, the one I'd found underneath the Sinclair family Bible. *As for Me and My House* by Sinclair Ross. I handed Grandma the book.

"This is where the name came from, right, Grandma?"

"Goodness, I'd forgotten about that," she said picking up the book and turning it over in her hands. "Well, I needed a married name. I was reading this when I went into labour. My name was Emma Sinclair. The author's name was Sinclair Ross. Sinclair and Ross.

"Ross was a good Scots name, and I needed to invent a red-headed Scots father just in case Susan came out ginger, which she did. So I told the hospital I was married and that my husband had left to fight in the war. And I'll tell you something for free," she said, turning to my mom. "I'd do it all again, Susan. I would have done anything, absolutely anything, to keep you with me."

My mom's head shook side to side as if she was answering no to a question no one had asked. "What did your parents say when you told them?"

"Tell my parents? Not in a month of Sundays! Scotch Gully — and that included my father — was in wholehearted agreement with the government of William Lyon Mackenzie King. My father believed all unwed mothers were fallen women and should never be entrusted to raise a child. He would have made me give you away, Susan."

My head spun like a funnel cloud. "That's horrible!" I said. I got up and wrapped my arms around my mom. "I know what it feels like to learn your own father didn't want you."

"But he did want you, Aunt Susan."

Everyone turned to look at David. "It's in Harry's letter. Harry, read it to her." David caught Harry's eye. "It's okay," David said. "It won't matter to Lizzie. She'll be fine with everything, I promise."

I didn't understand, but I trusted him.

"Are you okay with all this, Lizzie?" Harry asked when he'd finished reading the letter. "Are you okay about Archie and me?"

"Sure." I shrugged. "But . . ."

"But what?" my grandmother demanded.

"But we'd better make sure Bethany's gran doesn't find out. She *adores* Harry. She thinks he's the best, most perfect person in town. If she finds out about Harry and Archie, her head will explode."

Everyone, my whole family, laughed. Even Expo let out a happy howl.

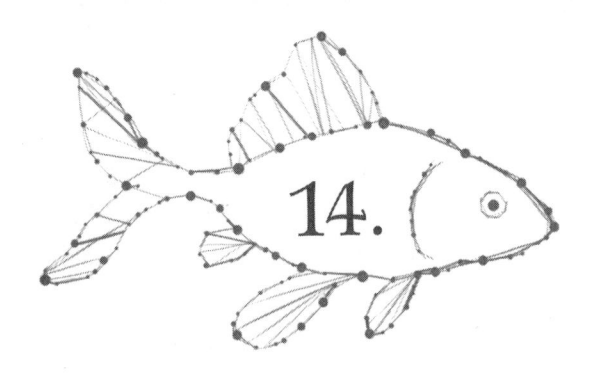

14.

Lizzie

We took two cars to Parents' Day — that's how big our family was now. Mom, Aunt Carla, David and I were in one car, with Grandma and Harry ahead of us in my grandmother's old Cortina.

"Is this normal?" Aunt Carla asked. "It looks like the whole town is here." She was right. The parking lot was almost as busy as it was on Field Day.

"Welcome to Scotch Gully," Mom said. "These things are always crowded, but tonight is special. By now, the whole town knows you're here, but not everyone has met you yet."

Aunt Carla rolled her eyes. David said, "Cool," but his attention was somewhere else. His nose was pressed against the window, and his right leg jiggled up and down. He was waiting for someone.

"Do you have butterflies, Lizzie?" Aunt Carla asked.

I was proud my project had been chosen, along with Gordon McInnis's, to be presented today, but I was nervous too. I'd spent my whole life trying to stay under the radar so that no one in town would have a reason to talk about my family. Now here I was, about to stand up in front of all of them and tell them things about us that not even old Mrs. Budge could have dreamed up on her most spiteful day.

"Butterflies? More like a charm of hungry hummingbirds," I said. "What if . . ."

Mom turned around to face me. So did Aunt Carla.

"I'm not embarrassed by our family," my mother said. "How about you, Carla?"

"Not one bit," she said. "I think we're pretty great."

I thought so too. It didn't bother me a fat tick that Harry and my grandfather loved each other. David wasn't bothered by it either. As for the rest of my family, it turns out Grandma had known for ages, ever since Aunt Carla was born. Grandma had been broken-hearted when Archie started another family, and Harry felt that telling her about him and Archie would be a kindness. As okay as I was with everything, I knew that coming out to the town about Grandma, Archie and Harry was going to cause a commotion way, *way* bigger than me having an unmarried mom. And that was something old Mrs. Budge had been feasting on for years.

Mom put the car in park. She asked, "Do you have your notes, Lizzie?"

"Here," David said, handing them to me with a strange sort of smile. I didn't get to ask him what his smile was for, because just then the Budgemobile pulled up beside us, with none other than old Mrs. Budge herself sitting in the passenger seat. A grin split David's face in half.

"She's here!" he cried and was out the door in a flash, his backpack bouncing as he ran. Bethany jumped out of the Budgemobile and ran toward David.

The two of them becoming friends sure had been a surprise. It had started on the way to school on David's very first day. He was sitting beside me on the bus when Gordon McInnis called over, "Hey, new kid. Are you coming out for hockey next fall?"

Scotch Gully is small, so getting a peewee and bantam team with two full lines of players was a big deal.

"I dunno," David yelled back. "I've never played hockey."

Bethany Budge was sitting in the seat in front of us, alone. She whipped around and barked at David. "Don't yell in my ear!"

"Sorry." David looked sheepish.

"So, kid, can you skate?" Gordon called, ignoring Bethany like he always did. But David couldn't ignore her — she was still turned backward in her seat, glowering at him as if daring him to yell again. David nodded his answer to Gordon, who pumped the air with his fist. "That'll make thirteen players. Two full lines and two spares."

"Can you really skate?" I whispered to David.

"Yeah. Grandad taught me. We'd take the tram to High Park and skate on Grenadier Pond."

"But do you want to play hockey?"

He shrugged. "I dunno. I guess I could try."

"No. Try not. Do . . . or do not. There is no try." Bethany said in a strange, strangled voice.

David's eyes popped. He leaned forward. I was a gnat's wing-flap away from warning him, "Don't touch her. She bites," when, in that same strange voice, David answered, *"Luminous beings are we, not this crude matter. You must feel the Force around you; here, between you, me, the tree, the rock, everywhere, yes."*

I should have seen this coming. Hockey was the number one item discussed by the boys on the school bus, but it was followed closely by anything Star Wars, even though it had been a whole year since the last movie came out. In our school, Bethany was famously nuts for Star Wars. Head-over- heels crazy. She wore her hair in Princess Leia ear-buns, talked like Yoda, and for two years, I'd heard her try again and again to join the boys in their Star Wars talk. They wouldn't let her. "You're a girl," they'd say, like that made a difference. And maybe that was their reason — maybe they didn't think girls and space stuff went together — but it could have been because she's . . . well . . . she's Bethany.

But David didn't know what she was like, and on that day, Bethany didn't know that David's mom was like my mom — unmarried. If she had known then, I'm pretty sure a lifetime of conditioning from her gran would have kicked in and Bethany would have growled at David like she did at me. Instead, Bethany and David happily talked Star Wars the entire bus ride to school, and after that — *BAM!* — Bethany was hooked. They became super-friends, and nothing her gran said after that could convince her that David was bad.

"So did you bring them?" she asked.

"You bet," David said, lifting his backpack. It was full of his collection of Star Wars action figures. Bethany had been dying to see them.

"Let's go," she said. The two of them ran for the gym door. Partway there, David stopped and called back, "You'll do great, Lizzie."

Then old Mrs. Budge walked right up to my grandmother, her purse dangling from her elbow. In a voice pitched loud and high, she quoted scripture. *"Lying lips are an abomination to the Lord.* Proverbs 12:22. You remember that, Emma Ross, the next time you come to church. You remember that."

"Now look here, Eileen," Harry said, and for a second, old lady Budge looked abashed. Like I said, she adored Harry.

Grandma put a hand on his arm. "It's fine, Harry." Then Grandma turned to old Mrs. Budge and said, "I expect you've heard the rumours, Eileen. Well, they're true. Susan is Archie Macrath's daughter. And yes, I lied about that. What's more, I'd do it again if it meant keeping my baby girl. If anyone in this town should understand that, Eileen Budge, it's you. I respected the choice you made all those years ago. I really hope you can respect mine."

Just then, I felt my mother grab my elbow and guide me gently away and toward the gym door.

"What did Grandma mean?" I asked when we were out of earshot. "Did Bethany's gran have a baby that was taken away in that adoption mandate?"

"I don't know, Lizzie," Mom said. "But if she did, it's her business. There's nothing to be gained by speculating. It will only fan the flames. Eileen Budge is an angry woman. Don't let her anger infect you. Look at Bethany."

We were inside the gym now. Mom nodded

toward David and Bethany. They were sitting on the chairs set out for today's presentation. They'd left an empty chair between them. On it, David had poured out his collection of action figures. Bethany picked each one up and admired them in turn. I was okay with them being friends now. And not just because it made my life easier.

"Bethany used to pick on you a lot, didn't she?" Mom asked.

"Ever since kindergarten. She hated me."

"She couldn't hate you, Lizzie. She barely knew you then."

"She sure acted like she hated me."

"That's because someone taught her to hate." We both knew who that was. But neither of us needed to say it out loud. "Hate isn't natural, Lizzie. It's learned. Look at Bethany now," Mom said. "She's not angry anymore, is she? David has shown her how to love."

My eyes popped wide.

"Not that kind of love," Mom chuckled.

Thank goodness. That would be one crazy-weird Thanksgiving dinner if David and Bethany ever fell in love. I tried to imagine both our families sitting around the dining room table with my grandma at one end and old Mrs. Budge at the other. Yikes.

* * * *

Gordon McInnis finished his presentation, and everybody clapped. Then it was my turn. When Miss G called out my name, it got so quiet in the gym, you could hear a frog fart.

I grabbed my presentation, stood up and edged my way past Grandma and Harry, Mom and Aunt Carla. David was still sitting in the back row with Bethany. As I scooched past, Aunt Carla reached out to stop me. With one finger, she beckoned me closer. "Nervous?" she asked.

I was. That charm of hummingbirds was flapping overtime in my belly. I'd thought I was okay with all this, but I wasn't so sure anymore. I'd spent a lifetime trying to go unnoticed, trying not to give folks reason to gossip and judge. Yet here I was about to stand up in front of the entire town and load the gossip gun for them.

Even with my whole family's support, as I climbed those wooden risers to the stage, it felt like there were lead weights in my shoes. My throat was dry. My hands felt shaky. I looked out over the crowded gym and found Harry. He nodded. Then, in the back row, David stood up and mimed that I should start reading.

David was right. I unfolded my notes, and there, on the front page in orange pencil crayon, was the outline of a fish — a goldfish with the letter *L* inside.

I looked up. David was still standing, grinning at me. I grinned back. I couldn't help it.

I began reading.

"When Miss Gambacort assigned this project, she told us that history wasn't just dates and places in a textbook or an encyclopedia. She said history happened *to* people, and there was a hero in every family. I didn't believe it could be true about my family. I was certain their lives had been dull and uninteresting. Boy, was I wrong! I had no idea what life was like for them. Wait till you hear."

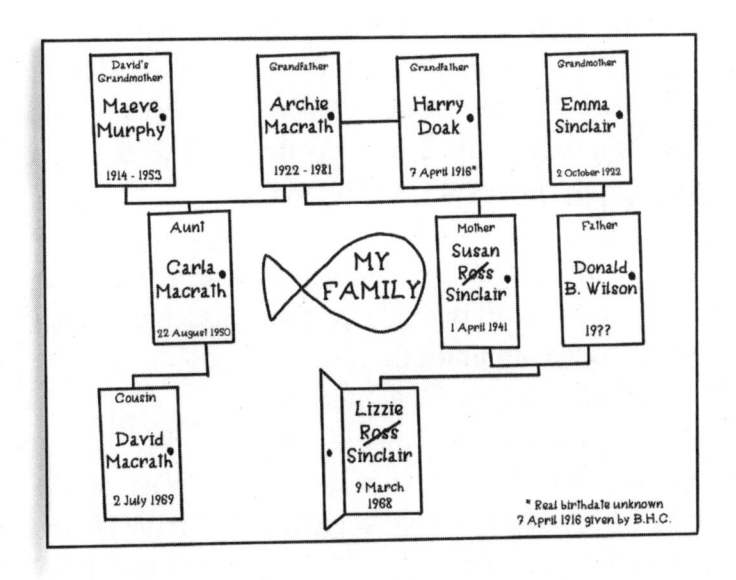

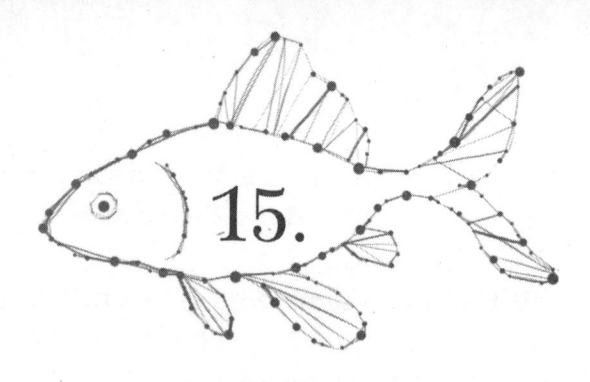

15.

And today . . .

David still lives on the Macrath Farm with his wife, Bethany (yes, *that* Bethany). They have three grown children and two grandchildren. They are happily planning a trip to the San Diego Comic-Con for their thirtieth wedding anniversary. David will be Han Solo from *The Force Awakens* — the one where he's killed by Kylo Ren — and Bethany plans to be General Leia Organa.

And Lizzie . . . ? Well, Lizzie is working to make the world a kinder place one story at a time (and her cousin is still the only person who laughs at her weird sense of humour).

And in case you're wondering . . .

• David was right about those Star Wars action figures being valuable someday. In 2019, Hake's Auctions in York sold a 1979 prototype *Star Wars* Boba Fett for $185,850. A pre-release Boba Fett action figure like David's, in mint condition, can be worth as much as $45,000. Take that, Cameron Kelch!

- Speaking of Kelch, despite everything Kelch claimed to know about history, British home children are very real, and everything Lizzie told David about them is true. Today, a full ten percent of Canadians are descended from a British home child.
- The demonstration that David sees on Yonge Street at the beginning of the book is like the many protests and rallies that happened after the police raids of bathhouses known as Operation Soap, and the continuing police brutality against gays and lesbians. There really was a large demonstration, but it took place in June 1981, one month after David and Lizzie's story. Thanks to the efforts of many determined and caring people, Ontario added sexual orientation to its Human Rights Code in 1986. It would be another ten years before Parliament added the same rule to the Canadian Human Rights Act.

Acknowledgements

Thank you to my dad, Thorbjorn (Tom) Thorbjornsen, who showed me what happens to pet-store goldfish when you release them into a cottage pond.

To Elizabeth Bennett, Super-Agent, who believed in a quiet book about kindness and courage.

To my lovely, *lovely* editor, Anne Shone, and the entire team at Scholastic Canada: Andrea Casault, Stella Partheniou Grasso, Maral Maclagan, Nikole Kritikos, Diane Kerner, Gui Filippone. I can't imagine a nicer first-book experience. You're all quite wonderful. An extra special thank you to Julie McLaughlin, whose amazing cover art is absolutely perfect (I love the rainbow). Scholastic Canada rocks!

To Barbara Joan Scott, brilliant author, editor and friend, I am so lucky to have you as my trusted reader.

To writing coach Julie Artz, for being the Jiminy Cricket on my shoulder and for never letting me take shortcuts.

And to Alexia Roy, a talented friend who listens and laughs with me and can also make beautiful websites and family trees.

First books pass through many, *many* hands on their way to finding an agent and publisher. This book was fortunate to have had many early readers with pithy insights. Thank you to my young beta readers, Beatrice Norton and the Price kids: Addison, Ara and Cyrus. Your insights and reactions helped refine and polish. To Hillary Fazzari, Gwen Goodkin, Rina Nichols, Elisabeth Norton, Katia Novet Saint-Lot, Cindy Roorda, and Geoff, John, and Katherine Warren. A special I'm-forever-grateful thank you to fabulous middle-grade authors Angela Cerrito and Sheila Averbuch, for your generosity and for convincing me Goldfish was ready to query. To SCBWI for their workshops and webinars where Goldfish met Elizabeth Law, whose First Pages critique provided encouragement and enthusiasm exactly when I needed it. And to my writing community all over the globe — you know who you are. I couldn't have done this without you. I wish I could mention every last one of you.

And then there are the amazing people who shared their special knowledge and support. Thank you to Suzanne Raymond, for her story of chickens flying into trees and what she and Joanne had to do to get them back down again. Flashlights were involved! To Rose Schumacher, my uber-talented quilting pal and experienced sheep farmer, for her help with all things ruminant. Rose sent me videos and even phoned other sheep farmers on my behalf to make sure I had accurate info. Rose, you are a star! To fantasy author Laura "Awesome" Rueckert, who stepped up with research about verbal anachronisms.

To chickens Alice and Nugget, RIP.

And to my oh so wonderful family — Freddie, Gabou, Puffin, John, Mic and Geoff. You put up with me and all my weirdnesses. I am so very lucky that you're mine. I love you.